D0928007

DEANDRE KRALEVIC

WARZONE
The First Mission

outskirts
press

Warzone
The First Mission
All Rights Reserved.
Copyright © 2022 Deandre Kralevic
v1.0

This is a work of fiction. Names, characters, businesses, places, events, locales, and incidents are either the products of the author's imagination or used in a fictitious manner. Any resemblance to actual persons, living or dead, or actual events is purely coincidental.

The opinions expressed in this manuscript are solely the opinions of the author and do not represent the opinions or thoughts of the publisher. The author has represented and warranted full ownership and/or legal right to publish all the materials in this book.

This book may not be reproduced, transmitted, or stored in whole or in part by any means, including graphic, electronic, or mechanical without the express written consent of the publisher except in the case of brief quotations embodied in critical articles and reviews.

Outskirts Press, Inc.
http://www.outskirtspress.com

ISBN: 978-1-9772-4908-1

Cover Photo © 2022 Deandre Kralevic. All rights reserved - used with permission.

Outskirts Press and the "OP" logo are trademarks belonging to Outskirts Press, Inc.

PRINTED IN THE UNITED STATES OF AMERICA

PREFACE

I t is 6:30 a.m on a warm summer morning in Milwaukee, Wisconsin. Dr. Maria Gonzalez is already awake, in the office, coffee made. She has been working on a masterpiece for a groundbreaking microchip that would offer the United States military a huge advantage when it comes to nuclear warfare. With the advancement in nuclear weapons since 2023, the likelihood of someone finally dropping a bomb somewhere is more of a where than a when. It is 2028 and Dr. Gonzales has reached the pinnacle of her design.

She calls it her baby. It is a microchip that, once activated, allows the user to absorb all nuclear power within 100 meters. The only way to release the power once stored is by destroying the entire chip. The United States is currently having her design the chip to survive a flight attached to a live missile either housed on a Black Hawk, AC-130, or a B-2 Stealth Bomber. The object is to attach the chip to one of the missiles and launch it once the missile makes impact as a nuclear explosion. Working through most nights she has finally completed the project; it is now ready for testing; she believes it will work properly on the first test run.

She sets her John Hopkins University mug down onto her desk. Somewhat OCD, her desk is so clean that a speck of dust would seemingly pop out like neon lights in a dark alley. She rearranges her coffee mug until it is perfectly lined up with the top of her keyboard. As soon as she begins typing, she notices that there are ripples moving through her coffee as though the desk underneath it is slightly vibrating, but she feels nothing. That was odd. Adjusting the mug again, this time she feels a tremor herself. Frightened by the sudden quiver of the Earth, she rises and runs to the window to have a look. Her office is on the top floor of the Clinical Laboratory Science building located in Marquette University. She can not believe her eyes, approaching the city from above are about 50 to 100 soldiers gliding in on military grade parachutes. "What the hell is going on?" she says out loud mostly to herself. Then she hears the roar of fighter jets overhead followed by the sickening explosion of missiles landing in the city around her.

The next noise is the blasting siren, mostly used during tornado warnings, but clearly it is being used to signal evacuation and an attack on the city. But why Milwaukee? Her answers are soon to be answered by four loud thuds on top of her roof. She can hear men moving around above her. What do they want? She hears the zipline being attached to the side of the roof closest to her window. The noise of boots landing on the side of the building is like a build-up to the worst climax in a scary movie. CRASH! Glass flies into the room and covers the lab's office floor, some spilling underneath the desk where Dr. Gonzales hides. She tries her best to be quiet, but her biggest fear is answered when the intruder speaks. "Она здесь, и я хочу ее живой." She knows that language, and by the sound of his accent she knows that he is Russian. "She's here, and I want her alive." Why do they want her? Before she can stop herself, her pride will not let her cower anymore. She stands up and reveals her position to the intruder.

"Ah, there she is." This time the intruder speaks in English. "Стук ее, и принести ее с собой!" he orders to his team. "Knock her out?" she thinks, "Bring her with us?" Her anxiety shoots up, and that's when she realizes it is too late for her to fight. Someone had approached her on the left and managed to stick a needle into her arm. Her consciousness is fading. Before blacking out completely she notices that the man takes his mask off and to her surprise, he is American.

Part 1

The Elite 5

"The object of war is not to die for your country
but make the other bastard die for his."
-General George S. Patten

1

"It's another 100-degree day here in the great city of Kyle, TX," exclaims the radio broadcaster. Dee wakes up from his nap, rubs his sleepy eyes and glances at his alarm clock.

"Shit," he mutters as he stumbles out of bed; the old radio alarm clock shows 10:55 a.m. He stumbles over to the bathroom for his morning routine before hitting the gym. As he's washing his hands, he peers up into his clean over-the-sink mirror and does not like what he sees. Curly unkempt hair that almost resembles sheep's wool if it were jet black. The 5 o'clock shadow looks like an end-of-day stubble and itchy too. "Babe, I am so sorry, I overslept, and you didn't wake me. Are the kids at school?"

"Yes! No thanks to you," she yells back. "This is the third day in a row I receive no help getting them ready." She enters their bathroom and sits on the toilet. She is stunningly beautiful. Eyes are blue as the clearest southern sky, perfectly framed by thin black coach glasses. Her dirty blonde hair is in its normal messy high bun when dealing with the five little ones in the morning. She signs, "Dee, I don't know what's going on with you, but I am going to need your help; this shit is hard by myself."

Dee reaches down, lifts her head in his damp palm and lightly kisses her on the forehead, "It won't happen again, babe, I promise."

"Good," she says with a faint smile. "I didn't make them by myself, so I ain't raising them by myself."

Dee walks out of the bathroom, leaving his wife in there so she can finish her business alone. "Babe, do you think I need a haircut?" Dee asks while looking in the body size mirror that his wife insists they need for their room.

"Yes, please!" she calls. "I didn't marry a cave man; I sure don't want to keep waking up to one."

He laughs, it was such a low pitch, that it seemed to be more of a growl than a laugh. "Okay, after I leave the gym, I'll head to the shop and clean this up."

Dee Jackson is 6'1" and is packed tight with muscles. When he walks by, he seems to cast shadows on others as he passes them. Being only 6'1", he is not a very tall man, but the sheer size and the presence that he carries around can fill a room. People on first impression assume he is a hard ass. Someone not to bother unless you absolutely have too. Those people would be right. Dee lives by the code, only the strong survive and his demeanor with everyone besides his family feels that.

Working out is not just a hobby of Dee's but his way of living as well. He is a well-known fitness instructor at the local Gold's Gym just across the bridge from RM 150 in the adjacent lot from H.E.B. He drives a hard ship when it comes to his weight training, even for his clients. He only accepts the truly dedicated and he can sometimes tell just by looking at them if they won't make it. Jackson is an Army veteran, 13 tours to Afghanistan and Syria while with the 75th Ranger Battalion and four covert operations when he joined the superior Delta Force. Eleven years of service to his country and he misses it every day. Though he was only 28 years old his wife finally says enough is enough. That meant it was time to call it quits. He is now in the reserves, teaching and training new recruits at the Ranger School in Fort Benning, GA, on a four-month rotation with the current staff.

Since he is running late, he doesn't have time for a shower, knowing he can shower at the gym. He quickly grabs his packed gym bag from under the bed while throwing on his usual black joggers and sleeveless "Lead the Way" hoodie. "Call me if you need anything babe; I'll be back in time to grab the kids from school!" he calls as he runs out of the door, eager to get to his place of peace—his second home.

Walking through his home, he notices that everything seems to be in shambles. His children really do give his wife a hard time. Feeling a little guilty, he stops to jot down a quick note for his wife to find later: "I will make dinner tonight, no help, just me. Sorry about this morning. Love you, Dee."

Feeling a little bit better he grabs his car keys off the "Home" key rack. Another item from Hobby Lobby that his wife just "had" to have. He adjusts his bag over his shoulder and opens the front door.

The radio broadcaster is not lying. It is 100-degrees or over. If you look closely, you can see the waves of heat coming off the pavement just waiting on you to drop your breakfast to instantly fry whatever it was that you were eating. When he enters the heat wave, he instantly begins to sweat. Damn it! Why was she so set on moving here; it's so fucking hot.

His neighbor, a scrawny pale man with wire-framed glasses and unnaturally long arms stops his lawn mower and yells, "Howdy Jackson, it's a hot one today innit?"

Jackson looks up at the man with total disdain on his face, "Clearly, you fucking dumbass." he mutters and gets into his vehicle. Dee drives a nice 2026 "Blacked Out" edition Range Rover Sport–575 horsepower, 5.0 L V8 engine, fully loaded and not a speck of dirt anywhere on the slick black exterior. It has become his ritual to start his SUV and listen to the engine purr before leaving for the day. Waiting until his neighbor looks away, he guns it away from his house startling the man and causing him to tumble over his rake. As he is driving down the road, he cranks the AC to max and turns on the radio.

A live bulletin interrupts what seems to be an old school Da Baby hip hop song on the station. "According to live reports from Milwaukee, Wisconsin, citizens are being evacuated as we speak., exclaims the broadcaster. The city is under attack from live airstrike attacks and active shootings." Dee pulls his SUV to the side of the road and turns up the volume on the radio. The reporter continues, "Milwaukee, news are actively reporting that an army of unknown combatants have parachuted into the city and are firing at and taking citizens hostage."

Sitting back in his seat, glaring out of his driver seat window, he suspects that today may be the last day that his family sees him for a while. He's ready for the argument and lack of understanding he will face once he explains to his wife that he will be boots on the ground again. He turns the sleek Range Rover around and heads back home.

2

The gym is cold, Gold's always has their AC turned on max when the temperature outside is torching the Earth. Scott looks down at his watch–11:19 a.m., "Jackson is never late, what the hell?" Standing in front of the gym, he finally heads back to the locker room to change into his workout gear. Muscles throbbing and fingertips tingling, Scott is scooping his pre workout into its measuring cup and dumping it into his mouth, chasing the grainy powder with a whole bottle of water. The thought of ripping Jackson a new one plays into his mind over and over again, because he knows what it is like to waste precious minutes when the "boost" is kicking in.

Scott Horner is an old Marine veteran--not just any Marine he would tell you--but an Elite Marine. Gunnery Sergeant (GySgt) Horner was a part of what is rumored to be the best sniper group in all of the military, a Scout Sniper for the Force Recon Marines. Still serving, taking leave is a must if you ever want to see your family. So, he is doing exactly that. A part of his family is his best friend, Dee Jackson. They met on a tour in Afghanistan, where Scott and his spotter were assigned to work with the Delta Force. Initially, he thought that Jackson was an asshole, and that any moment he would end up getting into a physical altercation. However, it played out differently when Horner was the person that saved Jackson's life. Two critical sniper shots killed an al-Qaeda member planting an Improvised Explosive Device (IED) on the road 300 meters from Jackson's Humvee and shooting the actual device, causing it to detonate before Jackson's fire team reached the kill zone.

Horner is just as much of a physical specimen as Jackson, standing 6'3," boasting an impressive 221-pound physique. The gym allows him to work out shirtless, no one else knows why he gets the special treatment, but many assume that they are afraid of him and Jackson. "Excuse me, honey," he says flirtatiously to the front desk attendant, "If you see Jackson coming in here, tell him to take his ass back out the door." The young woman, is extremely attractive. Short, probably around 5'1" if he had to guess, tight body, spicy attitude, and seductive green eyes. She replies smiling, "Now, Mr. Horner, why would I go and tell him to do that, he's my favorite trainer." "Wow, straight for the instant kill, aye? Ooh rah!" he says chuckling as he walks away toward the free weight section of the gym.

This was his heaven, the unavoidable stench of sweat, the loud clang of the metal barbells being re-racked after someone finishes a set, the echoing thud as the rubber weights drop over and over again from someone completing reps power cleaning. Scott was not like most guys that hit the gym, he was in love with leg day. He had thighs as thick as tree trunks and calves the size of MLB baseballs. Today was no different than any other Friday, it was leg day. Making his way to the squat rack, he passes by a member of the gym's private trainers.

"Yo, Marine" called the trainer, "have you seen Dee? He hasn't come in yet." "What's up Chris, nah man, I haven't seen or heard from him yet," returns Scott. Chris looks as though we wanted to ask another question, but Scott keeps walking as if he had nothing more to say.

Reaching the squat rack he grabs the metal frame, "Finally here, baby, let's put some work in," whispers Horner. Loading up the bar with 200 pounds for warming up, he sinks into the squatter's position. Exhaling and inhaling at the pace of a woman giving birth, he removes the bar from the frame. "Ass to grass baby, ass to grass," he repeats to himself. He easily hits 15 repetitions before he re-racks the bar with his favorite loud clang and begins to immediately add weight to the bar. Adding 75 more pounds to the bar, Scott retakes his position under the bar. He repeats his mantra, "Ass to grass baby, ass to grass." After 20 repetitions, he reracks the bar and reaches for more weight. He looks in the mirror while picking up a 45-pound plate and notices three new guys watching him. He puts the plate on and turns and looks at the group smiling, "You like what you see young'uns?" The men immediately go back to what they were calling working out. One man lifting, while the other two stand around bullshitting. Walking to the other side of the rack he shakes his head. And they wonder why they never see any gains. On the rack sits 365 pounds, just 35 pounds from his personal record. He grips the bar, gets into position for the third time, and lifts the bar off the rack. "Oooh wee, this muthafucker is heavy today!" he blurts out. He inhales and exhales three quick times before beginning his repetition. The veins in his face and his neck are bulging to the point, where if you did not know him, you'd think he is about to have an explosive eruption of blood. Completing his twelve reps, he re-racks the bar again.

Sweating so much, he needs a mop to dry his face, wipes his hands on his towel and begins to add fifteen more pounds. This time looking up in the mirror, he sees that sexy front desk attendant walking toward him. Shit, what's her name again? "Ah, Sarah, what brings you over to the foxhole." he asks clearly trying to flex his abs. "Dee just called for you, he said it's urgent--to call him right away."

She does not even glance at his body. As he begins to follow her out of the weight room, he wipes the sweat off his face, "Did he happen to say what this problem was?" "Nope," she replied, "he just said to call him back." She returns to her post behind the desk and begins watching TikTok videos silently lip syncing the words to one of the videos.

Scott heads straight to the locker room, opens his locker, rummages through his bag, and locates his iPhone XXX. He picks the phone up and says, "Siri, call Jackass." The phone rings once before Jackson picks it up. "Horner, have you heard what's going on in Milwaukee, Wisconsin?" Dee asks quickly.

"Nah man, I haven't heard nothing, what's going on?" replies Scott, confused. "Man, if your old ass don't turn on the TV, look at the news, any channel!" cracks Dee.

Scott stands on the bench in the locker room, reaches up and turns the TV on. Instantly, he sees the news reports, "Live footage of foreign soldiers driving through our city, throwing what appears to be "fireballs" of some kind from the windows of the vehicles," yells out the male reporter. With the news still playing in the background, Scott asks, "Jackson, what the fuck is going on?"

"I don't know, brotha, but wheels up in forty-five minutes," growled Jackson.

3

"Hey man, do you see that right there?" asks Luper, pointing to the large trash pile on the side of the road. Petty Officer (PO) Luper and his Seal team are driving through the center of the Helmand River Valley in Afghanistan. "Dude, relax, this country is dirty as hell; there is literally trash everywhere." replies Chief Lewis the Seal Team 3 Leader. As the beat-up Toyota Tundra whips down the road, PO Luper shouts, "Nah, nah, nah Skipper, that specific pile was not there yesterday when we did our routes." Speeding so fast and the loud rattle from the old truck, Chief Lewis doesn't even hear the next warning from PO Luper, "IED! IED!" Luper jumps out of the truck followed by the two other members of his team who were sitting in back of the pickup truck. Not paying attention, Luper gets too close to the pile of trash in the road and the bomb goes off. BOOM! Huge explosion: gives you the feeling that the entire valley has just shook, all of the birds took flight and the loud whistle Luper had in his ear was enough to confirm that his Chief did not survive the blast. "Ambush!" screams another member of the team. The crackle of assault-rifle rounds shatters the silence, as if there is an invisible mirror around the three men.

Luper runs to get cover behind the only thing in the valley—which happens to be the burning cab of the Toyota they were just driving in. He begins to fire back, CRACK! CRACK! CRACK! The sound of his submachine gun is soothing; he knows this weapon better than anything he has ever operated. The only problem is that the target was on top of the valley looking down, and his HK MP5 K could not reach that distance, especially if he did not have a clear shot.

"Where are they?" Luper shouts.

"I can't see these slimy muthafuckers, man. Seems like they are every-fucking-where!" exclaims another member of his team. That was Scooter. He hates that name, so everyone just calls him Scoot. Brand new to the team, and his first fire fight. Welcome to the Suck. Scoot is lying down in the center of the valley behind what looked to be what's left of the engine block. He looks to Luper and signals that he is going to move up to the thin tree line just about 50 meters to his north. Luper nods to acknowledge that he will try to cover when he begins his movement.

Scoot takes off running before he dives into the tree line. At this moment Luper spots two men on top of the ridge one clearly holding an RPG and the other pointing to where Scoot just ran to. "SCOOT, RPG!!" screams Luper. It is too late; the RPG was fired before Luper could give the warning and the RPG sprays Scoot's bodily makeup all over the valley floor. This is a shitstorm.

Scanning the valley for the last member of his team, he finally spots another Seal member in the tree line. "Roaker, Roaker?" Luper calls out. He makes the number two symbol with his left-hand points to his own eyes, then points to the top of the ridge where the RPG was just launched from. Roaker looks up with his tricked out M4 and spots the two men with his scope. Fires two rounds, CRACK! CRACK! Both shots are straight on and both men fall down the ridge, lifeless bodies bouncing off the mountain before resting on the floor of the valley in the tree line. Luper gets up and begins to move toward Roaker. Roaker is the radio man, he has direct communication with command. They need help now.

The Petty Officer takes the radio from Roaker and begins to speak with a sense of urgency but in a calm, controlled manner to ensure that all commands are heard. "This is Petty Officer Luper; break,"

A voice responds back on the radio, "This is Wolves Den over."

Luper continues, "We have two men KIA, and we are in need of CASEVAC; break, we are pinned down in the middle of the Helmand River Valley; coordinates are as follows LAT 31.363647 LONG 63.958611; break. Black Smoke is the marker, break. Engaged with enemy. How copy? Over."

"Good copy, Luper, birds in the sky, five mikes out," replies the man on the radio.

Three minutes later the sound of their getaway chariots approach, one Chinook and two Black Hawks. While the Chinook pilot is trying to land the helicopter in the valley to collect what is left of the dead, the two Black Hawks are engaged with the Taliban on the ridge. You could hear the long wind up on the miniguns that are being fired into the ridge line while also hearing the loud whistle and explosion as the Hellfire missiles connect with multiple targets. "This is American power you fucking towel heads!" screamed Luper, "ambush that, muthafuckers!" As Luper and Roaker make a run for the Chinook in the valley, an RPG connects with the back side, igniting the helicopter and grounding it for good.

"What the fuck!" yells Roaker behind him.

"FUUUUCCCK!!" yells Luper as he jolts awake and sits up in his bed. Another nightmare from the worst day in his military career. His wife is up next to him, kisses him on the shoulder, "You're okay, babe, you're here with me." she says.

These nightmares have been happening for the past year, but Aaron Luper refuses to go talk to someone. "Hon, I know what you're thinking, I am just not ready to talk to a shrink yet, okay?" says Aaron without looking at his wife. He is embarrassed with himself; being as tough as nails does not stop your mind from beating you up from within.

Aaron Luper looks at the clock next to his bed, it is 8:19 a.m. in Fort Wainwright, Alaska. A place he had requested from his Commander where he could be stationed for a few months while recouping from the last visit to Afghanistan. Getting out of the bed and looking out of the window he could see that today was going to be a cold one. "Honey, I'm going to shower, then go see what I can get from the chow hall for breakfast. You want anything?" asked Aaron.

"No, my love," she says, "me and Emily will be going out today to look for the Giant Elk we saw yesterday."

"Be careful Sarah, those things are no joke," he says with a smile on his face.

After his wife and daughter leave the house, he gets into the shower. The soothing hot water and the steam seem to melt his anxiety away as if it were never there. Finally, relaxed enough to get out he turns off the water and steps out of the walk-in shower. Looking in the mirror he sees the scar that will haunt him for the rest of his life. Long, jagged scar where his own knife dug into his side when he jumped from the old Toyota that hell day in Helmand.

BANG! BANG! There was a loud knock on his front door. Dressed in nothing but a towel wrapped around his waist, Luper didn't boast a giant frame. He was only 5'11" and 190 pounds. All his Seal friends joke and say that Luper isn't big, and he is fucking skinny buff. Sharp blue eyes that pierce the soul of all enemy and make them regret wanting to die for their cause and a beard that a lumberjack would be proud of. He opens his front door, "What the hell Lupe? Let's go, man." says a guy that looks no older than 19 years old. "Give me a sec, Turner, let me put my uni on." Turner was a new member of Seal Team 3; Luper was not a fan of instantly replacing one of his old comrades, but it is a business, he always thinks. Just the same, he always wonders, "Why so young?" He comes out of his room fully dressed and carrying his hat, "Alright man, let's go." grumbled Luper.

"Skipper gave me strict orders to drive you to medical this morning, he wants you to talk to someone," says Turner reluctantly. Getting into the passenger seat, Luper freezes; Panic rises in his chest as he begins to hyperventilate. "Get the fuck out of the car!" Luper yells.

Turner jumps out and says, "What the hell, dude?"

"It's nothing, let me drive or I'm not going," replies Luper.

"Fuck it," replies Turner as he throws the keys to Luper.

On the way to the chow hall, Luper's phone rings. He answers, "Good morning, sir, I am on my way to the doc now."

"Sorry to tell you, Luper, but that will have to wait. Go talk to Sarah instead; we need you out of here in 45 minutes. You will be briefed on the bird." Luper hangs up and looks at Turner, "Has to be that shit that is going on in Milwaukee, Wisconsin, right?" says Turner.

Aaron stares blankly as he is driving back home. "What shit?"

4

She lays back on her pillow, smoking a cigarette after what she feels to be the best sex she has had in a long time. Looking to her left, she sees that her husband is passed out in the fetal position. She smiles to herself, the feeling of tiring out a fully grown man with an act that they believe they are superior in is a highly infectious feeling. She looks down at her own perfectly sculpted body, the beads of sweat that are slowly gliding down between her breasts. She knows she will have to change the sheets once he wakes up, she can feel them damp beneath her butt. She gets out of the bed and walks over to the picturesque view of the countryside of Atlanta, GA. It is 12:30 p.m., and it is already hot. The next-door neighbor is already out watering his lawn when he looks up to behold all of what is Georgianna, Georgi for short, is what she likes to remind people. She smiles and waves,

The man is taken aback by how bold she is in the huge window, showing everything that God has blessed her with. The man is not able to remove his eyes; he feels glued to her.

She notices him staring for the first time since she's been standing there, and she is instantly turned on by the fact that this man is transfixed by her. She begins to touch her body, with her cigarette in the corner of her mouth, she slowly begins to dance. She grabs her breasts and gently squeezes while the other hand ventures down south to an area that is so smooth it feels as though anything would slide completely away from its surface. The man next door begins to smile, he drops the water hose and moves a little closer to the fence. Georgi turns around and slowly bends over when she suddenly hears, "You fucking slut!"

She turns around and witnesses the man's wife outside pounding away at her husband with the handle of her broom. The woman then begins to yell at Georgi, but instead of entertaining the woman, she smiles and closes the shades of her window.

She's never had issues with her body or people watching or looking at her before, but she always gets the same response from women, "Whore!" "Slut!" "Crazy bitch!" She always tells herself that they are just jealous that men do not fall all over them as they do her. She's happily married anyway, but she just loves the attention. Georgi is 5'8" 168 pounds and everyone including her husband has always said that she is "thick" in the right places. Being 30 and still garnishing these responses from men of all ages is what keeps her in the gym and keeps her working to stay young.

Finally making her way to the bathroom, she notices that her phone has thirteen missed calls. Walking over to her phone, she realizes it's her squadron that's trying to call her. Never a break from work, and when she gets some down-time all she has time to do is work out and make love. She picks up her phone and brings it into the bathroom with her, starts her shower and hits redial on the missed call.

"Sgt Zelks?" asks the voice on the phone.

"Yes sir." replies Georgi. "We need you in the office ASAP, we have a situation in Iraq that we need you for. Be here at 1330 for your briefing and ready to take flight at 1400hrs. "Yes sir," she replies. She hangs up and jumps into the shower, she now must find a way to tell her husband that she has to leave again, and she just returned from Moscow yesterday.

Coming out of the shower she smells breakfast being made. Eggs, bacon, bagels, and coffee. She loves coffee but bacon is her true weakness. Feeling hungry but guilty all at once she quickly gets into her uniform, while tying her boots her husband enters the room wearing only slippers. "Made you breakfast G, after a showing like that earlier I know you're hungry."

"Damn, I just got called into work, love. I am heading out in an hour. So sorry, baby," she says, looking straight into his eyes. She can see his soul crumble through the windows that are his eyes, and she instantly feels terrible. It is always like this, but for some reason he sticks around. "It's ok, babe, take some for the road, consider it my payment for the effort you put in," he replies jokingly. She stands up, walks to him, and grabs him where he loves the most. "When I come back, I will definitely be charging you more," she says before kissing him. She releases him and heads to the kitchen to make herself a quick "to go" plate.

Her husband never asks her about where she is going or what her mission is; he just knows from experience that she cannot give him any details. It comes with the job, the secrecy, and she hates it. But it takes care of them and their daughters. After completing her plate and chomping a piece of perfectly crisp bacon between her lips she shouts her goodbyes and a quick "I love you" before she runs out the back door.

Sgt Georgi Zelks is a PJ, which is short for Pararescue for the United States Air

Force. She has been in the Air Force for seven years and finding it exceedingly difficult to progress in rank. She feels as though there is no other PJ that can compete with her in the field but because she is a woman, she is shortchanged on promotion every time. She scores high on her promotion exams but when it comes for selection, she does not get it. This time around she will get it or else she is out.

Pulling up to her command, she scarfs down the rest of her breakfast that she's eating in her car. She already sees the commander waiting outside the building. "God, so fucking pressed!" she says out loud to herself before getting out of her car.

Major Shaw is a good guy, work is his only passion seeing as how he's single and the only man resistant to her charm. She hurries out of her car and puts on her cap; walking over to him she silently counts how many missions she has completed and how many lives she has saved—26 missions and 122 lives that she's personally saved. Jumping behind enemy lines and providing first aid and evacuating allies is her specialty. That is the job of a PJ and she does it better than anyone. Major Shaw meets her halfway up the walkway and turns around to match her stride into the building. "Okay Zelks, here's the info, we have thirteen American hostages inside of a compound that is currently garrisoned by ISIS. The Marines have the building surrounded and ready to breach but they are afraid that if they breach it will create danger for the hostages."

Sgt Zelks nodded and posed her own question, "Do we know if the hostages are all in the same room, or are they spread out?"

"Well, what we know is there are thirteen of them." Major Shaw begins, "but we do not know if they are being kept together or if they're separated? That's your teams' job to find out," states Shaw. "Your team has been briefed and ready to take off." said Shaw as another airman comes running down the flight path.

"Sir, we just got a call from the Pentagon; Sgt Zelks is being requested in D.C right now." Shouted the extremely exhausted airman. The airman hands the commander the secure phone he is carrying and stands at the position of at ease while he makes the call back. "Major Shaw here, can I request of what importance is this mission you need my airman for?" he said.

"This mission is code word clearance only, Shaw--this is General Ratliff, and the President of the United States has selected Sgt Georgianna Zelks for this operation. There is a helio in-bound to you now to get her here. Make sure she's on that bird, Shaw." Then he terminated the call.

Georgi stands there looking at Shaw as he gives the phone back to the airman and watches him sprint away from them back to the outpost on the runway. "Looks like you won't be going to Iraq after all, someone needs you more in Washington D.C.," announced Major Shaw.

Just then they hear the sound of a helicopter approaching the runway, and instantly they realize it is Marine One, the President's helicopter. The door opens and a Marine steps out and asks, "Are you Sgt Zelks?"

Georgi looks at Shaw and he nods. "Yes, I am."

"The Marine says, "We're here for you, your chariot awaits."

5

It is a packed day in sunny Canterbury Park in Shakopee, Minnesota. All the glamour that comes with horse racing is on display today. Darwin Splinter walks into the park with the expectations of winning himself some money. Horse racing is the fastest way to either lose a lot of money or gain a healthy sum. Today felt like the day he would win it all. Walking through the center lobby here at Canterbury, he notices all types of characters within the racing scene. You have the old timers, the people that grew up betting and raising the horses for these types of races, something to behold from the early 2000s. Then you have the new age, people who come here for the actual event, not that they will bet, but just to watch the horses and all their glory. Some of the stallions are pure bred, made for this moment while others, like the horse that intrigued Darwin, were merely pleasant surprises, trained when found mistreated by an old owner. Golden Chariot was the name of this one. Brand new to the racing scene and, matter of fact, its first race of its young career.

In the interviews, the owners have said they do not know its blood line or even if the previous trainers raced the horse at all. They made many comments, stating that the horse was a natural and that they would not bet against it. That is exactly the advice that Darwin loves to hear. Waiting in line to place his bet, he hears the conversations of the men in front of him, "This is a shoo-in, if you want to win some money you have to go with the favorite," says one of the men dressed as though this was not his first rodeo. Another man chimes in, "I understand what you mean, but the true earnings are when you bet on a horse that is in the center of the pack, more bang for your buck." Darwin thought that was an interesting point of view, however, he knew the real money was when you bet on the underdog, the horse that no one expected to win. Today, that horse is Golden Chariot.

Finally, it is his turn at the window. The teller asks, "Hey sweetie, you paying with cash for today's race?"

"Why yes ma'am I am, is there any other way to have it?" replies Darwin with a smile. She gives him a card to fill out; noticing that he can bet on more than one horse, he chooses to put all his money on the one he believes to be his winner. "Fifteen hundred on Golden Chariot?" she says, shocked, looking down at the card Darwin hands her. "You're the first one today that has chosen that beauty, 16/1 odds," she says, taking his money and shaking her head. She hands him his receipt and wishes him luck.

Darwin takes his receipt and heads into the field seating to try and find a spot where he can watch the race without anybody getting in his way. Looking up into the stands he realizes that is going to be a difficult feat today.

Standing only 5'11" he is not overly tall, but he holds a commanding presence that makes him seem as though he is much larger than that. Presenting a body that was nicely sculptured due to his military background and love for CrossFit, he gives off the vibe that he could definitely pose a threat to anyone looking for trouble. Why is he at the racetrack? He's an ultra-competitor and would rather die than lose but would also rather see an underdog win than a hundred pampered thoroughbreds. Maybe that's why he fought like hell on the battlefield.

He decided to go to the very top, the area that people in other sports would call the "nose bleeds." This way he could stand on the bleachers and see the track and not block anyone's view behind him. "The race will start in approximately fifteen minutes" came the announcement over the intercoms. Just then Darwin could see all the jockeys parading around the field. "Damn, those are some little guys," Darwin says to the man sitting next to him. The man looks at Darwin like he's an idiot.

"Well, guess your parents didn't teach you manners," snaps Darwin. The man ignores him still and lifts his phone to his face as if to simulate that he's too busy to talk to him.

"Asshole," mumbles Darwin as he turns back to the track to watch the horses and the Jockeys set up in their stalls. His horse was number 13 and wore golden straps and his jockey was wearing gold and red. "Alright, lucky number thirteen!" boomed Darwin.

The pitch around the track became as silent as he ever heard it since he entered. Everyone in their seats are anticipating the opening of the gates and the thundering herd of horses hitting the track. BANG! The gates fly open as the horses shoot from the stall like bullets leaving a rifle headed straight for its destination. Darwin's stomach drops, instantly in knots. He notices his horse rears up in its stall before the jockey regains control and comes out of the stall in dead last. "Shit! This isn't looking good already," groaned Darwin. He takes a seat next to the man who is still holding his phone up to his face. "Why are you even here?" Darwin asks. The man next to him shrugs and resumes looking at his phone. Darwin can hear the commentating from the announcers in the booth above him.

"Prancing Lady bursts out of the gates taking an early lead," he announces. "Followed closely by Shooting Stars in second and Magnificent Pharaoh only a few lengths behind in third," he adds. "Then comes the pack, Daisy's Champion, Spanish Road, Basking Rays, Dukes Anointed, and Benji's Billions!" the announcer bellows. "And in last behind the pack is Golden Chariot." he says. "Today is Golden Chariot's first official race. Trained by August Newt in Ireland and ridden by 26-year-old Chris Stanly," the man adds.

This is not looking good for Darwin, $1500 was a lot of money, he is feeling like he just made a big mistake. "Damn, should have listened to those guys in the lobby," Darwin moans. The announcer continues with his play by play of the race, "Prancing Lady is holding the lead a good four lengths away from the second place Magnificent Pharaoh. Spanish Road has joined the top three, just one length away from Magnificent Pharaoh." Darwin can feel the devastation of his poor choice rising in his throat like a bad choice of dinner the night of drinking.

"It's the last 250 meters of the race and Prancing Lady still holds the lead," shouts the announcer. "Holy crap! Take a look at this, Golden Chariot is making a move on the final turn, Chris Stanly is giving him the ride of his life, look at that intensity," booms the announcer. Darwin stands up with renewed excitement, "Holy shit, run god dammit, run!" he says, jumping up and down. The announcer in the booth stands up, grabs his microphone, and leans in with one hand on the windowpane and shouts, "Down to the home stretch, Prancing Lady is still in the lead but not by much, followed closely behind by Magnificent Pharaoh and Golden Chariot making his move on the outside." He continues, "This is going to be a close one, ladies and gents, Prancing Lady is looking winded but Golden Chariot looks as though he has fresh legs, look at Stanly work that horse!" It's going to come down to the wire, "Oh my God, can he do it, Golden Chariot is neck and neck with Prancing Lady, here is the finish!" bellows the announcer. "The winner is...."

BING *BING* "Shit!" Darwin jumped just as the horses cross the line. His work phone has just gone off and this is bad. He never got called when he was on leave, so this had to be important. He runs out of the stands to call back the number from his command.

"SGT Splinter here, I just received a call," says Darwin to the soldier on the other end of the line. "Roger that, sarge, let me transfer you to Sergeant Major's office." Darwin's heart began to race, why is the SGM calling him and especially on leave. He hadn't done anything wrong, and he's only been away from the base for five days of his 14-day vacation. The line picked up, and a man that sounded like he smoked two packs of cigarettes a day came unto the phone, "SGM Holmes speaking."

"Good morning SGM, this is SGT Splinter calling. I received a call from Staff Duty, and they transferred me to you," says Darwin.

"Ah, yes, SGT Splinter, we need you to come back to the unit. You have just been called to action by the Pentagon, I have no clue what's going on, but they called specifically for you."

"Like come again, SGM?" he replies, feeling a little confused. "Yes, dumbass that's exactly what I said," cracks Holmes. "Get your ass back on the first flight here," he continues. "Your ride to D.C. will be here at 1500 hours." As soon as he finishes that statement, Holmes hangs up the phone.

"Damn dude, why do you have to be a prick every time?" mutters Darwin to his now black screened phone.

Just as he is walking out of the park, he happens to look up at one of the TVs inside of the lobby. His horse has pulled it off--$1500 just turned into $25,500 in the final seconds of the race. He didn't even get to see the finish, but what does that matter? He would be able to hold the winnings. First thing he gets to spend his money on is a plane ticket back to Fort Bragg, NC.

Part 2

The Mission

*"It is an unfortunate fact that we can secure
peace only by preparing for war."*
-John F. Kennedy

6

After sleeping for what seemed like 30 minutes on the entire three-hour flight, Jackson did not feel rested. Something about airplanes just did not sit right with him, especially flying to this part of the United States. Finally able to step off the Boeing 747, Jackson feels that humid air of Baltimore, Maryland for the first time. Man, it was hotter here than home because of all this damn humidity. Jackson took his coat off and stuffed it in his bag. Scott and Dee ride the same flight to the East Coast. Might as well since they thought they were summoned by the same people to the same place.

Scott grabs his bag. Okay, so orders said get to the White House. How the hell do we do that without any type of proof that we were called here? Just then a blacked out GMC Yukon pulls in front of them. Two secret service guys get out of the SUV. One is tall, built like an NFL lineman with freakishly large hands, while the other was around the same height but weighed considerably less.

"This is an odd pairing," cracks Dee as the two agents reach out for their bags. "Whoa. Whoa, how do you even know who we are?" says Scott who is eyeing the big guy. The smaller agent replies with a hint of agitation in his voice, "He have been shown pictures of you guys, of course, and now you have confirmed it by personality comparisons as well." The big agent holds out his hand to Dee, "The name is Special Agent Locke, my partner is Special Agent Lewis. You must be Dee Jackson?" he says. Jackson reaches out and shakes SA Locke's hand, "Yes sir, and clearly this is my sarcastic sumbitch partner, Scott Horner," Dee replies nodding towards Scott.

The men hand over their bags to the agents and get into the back of the SUV. Once the agents get back into the front of the vehicle the SA Lewis radios in. "We have the package en route to eagles' nest," he says into the sleeve of his right arm. "So, why fly us into Baltimore instead of giving us a flight straight to DC?" asks Scott, looking out the window as the SUV merges onto I-95. "Commands orders," replies SA Locke. "Everyone that is coming here is coming by different means, you two arrived first."

Jackson looked into the rearview mirror directly at the agent and asked, "So, why us, why are we here?"

Instead of allowing SA Locke to answer the question, Agent Lewis replies, "All your questions will be answered once we get to the White House, until then just try to enjoy the scenery."

The race to the White House was not scenic at all, it was all freeway and trees for miles. Finally, once they arrived at Washington D.C., they could see buildings. The Washington that is shown on TV and the place they were driving through did not match up.

"This is D.C.?" asked Scott clearly not impressed at what he was looking at. "We have regular-looking areas just like everywhere else," replies Special Agent Locke. "Not all of D.C. looks like Penn Ave and the National Mall," he says as they are making their way past the Washington Memorial.

Both Dee and Scott are astonished at how what most people would consider lower class, or the "ghetto" is literally around the corner from the cornerstone of the United States leadership. Pulling up to the South Lawn of the White House the black SUV pulls through a gate that is manned by two security guards carrying automatic weapons and another sitting in the booth. Both agents show their credentials, and the security guard asks for the identification of the two men in the backseat.

Just then, Jackson's window begins to slide down and the security guard is at the window. He holds his hand out while Scott and Dee fish in their wallets for the IDs. Scott passes his ID to Jackson and he hands them both to the guard. He scans them both and his computer makes a chirping sound. "Alright, they are cleared," the guard states. He gives the men back their IDs and hands them each a red visitor badge as well. "Wear these in the building at all times. If you are caught without it, the agents inside will give you a really hard time." He gestures at the agents driving the vehicle. "That's enough, Michael, don't you have some coffee to drink or something?" asked Agent Lewis sarcastically. "We're already dealing with it," says Jackson, laughing as the SUV shot forward to the roundabout in front of the White House doors.

The South Lawn of the White House is vast, with the most perfectly groomed grass and manicured hedges. While also boasting what seems to be an infinite number of trees, a tennis court, swimming pool, basketball court, running track, and a huge circular fountain surrounded by red tulips and hyacinths. It looked exactly as the pictures captured it. Perfect! "Hey, I have had this question for years; I can finally ask someone that knows," Scott says, sliding forward so he is directly in the middle of the two agents in the front seats. "Why is there a huge gap in between the Big House and everything out here?" Agent Locke smiles as he replies,

7

Walking through the White House is a first for four members of the group, however, Aaron has been here before. He was awarded the Purple Heart and the Bronze Star award for his service in the fight against the Taliban just a year ago. It is one of his finest achievements but also one of his worst nightmares. Coming home from the war was a relief, but not having his friends and shipmates with him was among the worst feelings ever. Guilt is a silent killer if you allow it to dwell, and Aaron refused to let it bunk inside of his brain, at least consciously.

Arriving at the West Wing of the White House, the team passes by many offices including the vice presidents. No one was there, it was as though it was a ghost town. "Hey boss?" calls out Scott to the Agent. "Is it always this empty in here? I always pictured it packed with people hustling about." Without turning around the agent answered, "It usually is, but today everyone has been sent home." The entire group looked at each other all with the same thought. More cloak and dagger.

Turning the corner, they pass by the Roosevelt Room, the door is closed but Scott and Darwin both want to take a peek inside. "There is nothing in there right now, everything has been cleaned and placed perfectly," states the agent without turning around. Directly in front of them is the door to the Oval Office. There stands a single marine dressed in his Color Guard Dress Blues. Dark blue blouse with "blood" red trimming around the collar, down the front of the blouse along the line of the buttons, around the cuffs, and along the bottom of the blouse. The Marine's awards that they've acquired will be displayed across the left side of their chest with the medals hanging just above the trim of the upper left chest pocket. Displayed on the right side of the Marine's chest are his unit awards, three to be exact. These awards will be displayed in ribbon form but in a straight line just above the right pocket trim. The six shiniest gold buttons led down to the white belt wrapped around the waist on the outside of the blouse where it comes together with a gold buckle distinguished by the globe and anchor of the Marines.

The Marine's pants where so white, the white walls almost looked dingy when compared. His black dress shoes were literally polished to the point Scott could see his reflection. The marine sentry had excellent posture, stiff as a board, eyes forward with his hands crossed in front of him sitting directly above his belt left hand over his right.

The Marine did not even acknowledge the fact, that six people just walked into his view. Before reaching the door, the agent grabs a phone off the desk and dials, "Yes ma'am, Mrs. President, we are here." He puts the phone down, gestures for the group to follow him towards the door. At this time the Marine moves: three quick movements in succession and the door was open. "That has to be the best damn opening of a door I have ever seen, son!" said Scott with high praise for his fellow Marine. The sentry does not acknowledge the praise...simply stands there until the six of them are through the door and shuts it behind them, returning to his post. The Marine does not have a name tag, they are there as silent sentries, only making themselves known in a crisis that involves the President.

Entering the Oval Office is almost surreal. Looks exactly like it does on TV, so neat and put together, nothing out of place. The floor is covered with a giant blue rug that bears the Presidential seal directly in the center. Sitting on top of the rug are small couches that look to be the color of ivory burnishing and old school design. A couple of bookshelves line the wall near the desk where the President sits and works. On the walls are pictures showing the American flag in a watercolor design and on the other side of the three windows is a picture of Benjamin Franklin. Behind the heavy-looking oak desk are the three windows and directly behind the chair are the American flag and the Presidential flag.

The President is not in the room yet. She is coming down from the Residential area where she was dealing with a matter that pertained to her family before the group arrived. "Geez, I wonder what could be so important that they brought us directly in front of the Commander in Chief," states Darwin, looking as though he does not wish to be here. Before Jackson can respond, a door opens on the other side of the room and in walks the President of the United States. President Christian Thomas has an average build for a woman of her age. She is a natural beauty; you could tell that she is not much for makeup—only tolerates what they put on her face when in front of the camera. Her hair is blonde, but not the blonde that you see on California super models. This blonde is a modest, almost straw-colored tint— like hair that's brushed by the very cleanest dirt. It was in a perfect bun at the back of her head without a string of hair falling loose from the red band she decided to use today. She takes long strides and covers the distance from the door to the desk within seconds, then sitting down behind the desk. Just as the door closes, Jackson catches a glimpse of another Marine sentry. Just to the right of the Commander in Chief stands a secret agent, senses heighted with so many people in the room, ready to act if needed to protect the package.

"Good evening everyone, glad to see you have made it," says the President. "Let us get down to business, shall we? I am sure you're all itching to find out why I called you five down here to speak in private."

Everyone in the room perks up, and for the first time on this trip Scott does not speak. The President leans forward with an expression that shows she is about to speak with emphasis, "Here is the situation..."

8

"The United States is under attack. We believe it to be the Russians," states the President to the group, who was listening attentively. "By now, the whole world knows that we have invaders on our soil and we leaders have not emerged to say anything about it yet." The President continues her speech to the group except now she cannot contain herself to her seat anymore. Beginning to pace back and forth behind her desk, she continues laying out the scene, "We wanted to get the information out to a competent team before we address the country, wanted to rush you guys here in order to get a lead on the problem so I can brief world leaders that we have a plan."

The group of five looked around at each other. "Why us?" is surely going through all of their minds simultaneously. Neither of the group has any ties to each other besides Scott and Dee, and they all come from different branches of service. Even Dee is a veteran who still goes on missions and training for the DOD through the reserves and his Ranger Battalion. President Thomas abruptly stops pacing, turns to face the team and says, "You five have been selected because of your specialties and your experience. We believe that creating an elite group of warriors, we can surprise the enemy and catch them off guard."

Dee Jackson spoke up for the first time since arriving in Washington D.C., "Madame President, why couldn't you have just enlisted the help of the Seals or Delta Force to do this mission?"

The Commander in Chief looked down at her desk before she gave the answer, "I knew you guys were going to want this answer, well, the truth is this mission is off the books. Your commands know that you are here and maybe your families know a little, but other than that no one knows of your arrival." The President sits down in her chair again before stating, "There is obviously a lot of risk to this job, if anything were to happen to you this mission never existed." The group looks around at each other with the silent confirmation that they aren't going to get obvious military support when their boots touch the ground in Milwaukee.

"Okay, that's fair," began Jackson. "So, what exactly is the mission, and what is the plan to execute it in the least amount of time possible and the safest route possible?" Christian Thomas looks at the group with dread in her eyes and the team knows it is more serious than they thought. "The mission is to recover a nuclear scientist by the name of Maria Gonzales. She was kidnapped by the terrorists and they have taken her to a secure makeshift lab in Miller Park Stadium." She continues to look the team right in the face when she tells them the most serious part of the problem. "The issue is that this specific scientist was in the process of creating a microchip that could turn any missile into a nuclear weapon. It draws nuclear power from any surrounding source, attaches to a missile of your choice, and upon impact of the missile releases the nuke and bam! Chaos."

Scott stands up and whistles, "Jesus, so you're telling us that all you have to do is attach it to anything and on impact it is nuclear?"

The President nods and leans back in her chair with her hands folded across her stomach. "Now, you can see why we need a black op team to retrieve her and hopefully thwart the enemy as well. We have her design, so if it came down to saving her or the chip they currently possess; choose the chip. It is a matter of national security," she states with a look so empathetic that she almost seems inhuman. "So, let her die for the sake of a mistake the country made of having her create this?" asks Georgi with an obvious attitude.

"Her life or the life of millions," President Thomas shoots back.

"If you agree to this mission, a close friend of our presidency has offered something like a bounty for your service. I'm talking $25 million to split five ways.," states the President. "That's literally $5 million to each of you...and if you wanted an honorable discharge from your service to avoid this mission, I could arrange that as well."

The group looks around and clearly everyone is on the same page with accepting the mission and possibly becoming $5 million richer. The only catch is whether they will survive the mission. "If we say yes, when do we start the process?" asks Dee who seems to be the clear-cut leader of the team.

"You would start now; I have a dossier here with everything you need to know and we've assigned you code names along with anything that you need to get this thing done," says the President, standing up and walking around the desk. "If you succeed in this mission, the country will owe you more than we can ever pay but knowing that you saved a nation will be in your minds always."

President Thomas gave the green folder containing the information regarding the operation to Jackson, "You were selected to be this team's leader. You put people where they need to be and make the mission move as fast as you can. You make the tough decisions, you got that?" asks POTUS. "You will have Predator drone support for target identification and air strikes from what we will call Command. It will be our call sign; you will be reporting directly to me and my team of trusted officials." She glances around at the group. Pointing first at Jackson she continues, "Your call sign is DAAM." Then looking down the line at the rest of the team in order from Scott, Darwin, Aaron, and lastly Georgi, she assigns them code names. "You're Snipez, Delta, Zero, and Medic."

"Easy enough to remember. You will be flown immediately to the safe house here in D.C where you will gear up, pack extra supplies and get ready for deployment at the break of dawn." She is done. She walks toward the door through which she entered the room. When she gets to the door, the Marine guard on the outside opens it. Before walking out she turns around. "Once you get packed up and ready to head out, an SUV will bring you back to BWI, you will then be flown to Milwaukee on a Chinook to a lightly inhabited area just outside of downtown. Be safe, and may God bless you on this mission." The President walks out of the door and leaves the agent in the room with the five members of the black ops team.

"Alright, follow me through the door by which you guys entered into this office and we can make our way to the safe house." The agent moves through the doorway before they have a chance to reply to his order. Walking back through the White House feels like a dream, there is no way they could have just accepted a $5 million mission from the President herself. The team feels nervous but craving the action all at the same time. If the team had anything in common, it would be the fact that they were all adrenaline junkies.

Exiting the White House, the team is back on the South Lawn, the black SUVs are waiting at the edge of the steps, ready to whisk them to their new lair and turn them into super soldiers. Entering the vehicles--two in one truck and three in the other--they shoot off. Inside of both SUVs is the same message delivered by the driver, "No talking, no phones, or stopping. I am to take you there, and that's it." The team rides silently, ready to burst with anticipation of the new mission and what the dossier holds inside. A sticker on the outside of the folder that was handed to Jackson read, "Only open once inside of the safe house."

Not realizing time had continued to move while standing in front of POTUS, they arrived at the safe house located in Fredrick, Maryland at 10:29 p.m. It was in the middle of nowhere in a small lake cottage. Once the team all steps out of the vehicles one of them drives off, the other goes to the edge of the woods, stops, turns off its lights and remains there.

Itching to find out what is inside the folder, the team moves to enter the safe house.

9

nside the house is like no other cabin the team has ever seen. It is nice and cozy on the inside but also straight business. There are two interrogation rooms located on the back east and west wings of the cabin while the front serves as an operation command center. Located in the middle section of the cabin is a military style locker room. It is fitted with weapons and different urban and woodland uniforms.

"This would be a good time to get outfitted with what we need now. Find weapons that best suit the mission and you." states Jackson to the rest of the team. "Once we've finished loading ourselves up and packing for this mission, we will reconvene here in the command center and go over a plan." Jackson immediately begins flipping through the dossier. The rest of the team disperses through the cabin to select gear for the upcoming mission.

Jackson walks straight for the locker room area. He knows that the right weapons are a must, but he also knows comfortability plus protection is important as well. Walking into the locker room he is pleased to see that everyone else had the same thought. The entire five-person squad is going through the gear looking for items that suit them and the mission.

Georgi is first to select gear from the closet. "All black I think is the way to go in an urban area," she murmurs, after selecting her garments. Choosing what Jackson believed to be the smallest pair of shorts he'd seen, Georgi adds black leggings and tank top with that set. Also, she chooses a black bulletproof vest and combat boots. She picks up a few other things including a black headband and a pair of black mechanic gloves. "Well, I got what I need, I'll be back once I'm changed," says Georgi as she takes her armful of stuff and leaves the room to the guys.

Darwin chooses his gear next. Going with the all black scheme as well, he chooses: ski mask, utility pants, combat boots, a long sleeve Under Armour compression shirt, the same mechanic gloves and a bulletproof vest. Unlike Georgi, Darwin starts to change as soon as he walks away from the closet.

Scott is next in line; he goes all black as well but he goes conventional military attire. He grabs what looks to be a military uniform but all black. Only thing he does not pick up is the helmet. He decides to go with a black bandanna as well, putting his salt and pepper hair into a ponytail at the back of his head. "Jackson, I know you're old school like me, do you want this black uniform as well?" he asks looking back at Jackson who is waiting in the doorway. Jackson nods and says, "Get me one of those helmets too and a vest."

Scott picks up another set of the same uniform and a helmet for Jackson and walks out of the closet. "Here ya go, bud, this is what I am wearing into the action, but I'm going to head to the lake to see if I can secure some trash to make myself an urban ghillie." He hands the uniform to Jackson. "You know, just in case the mission calls for an invisible sniper." Scott says as he walks away smiling.

Aaron is the last one to walk into the closet and grab his gear. He chooses the same thing that Jackson and Scott are going with but also selects an Explosive Ordnance Disposal uniform as well. The EOD uniform is bulky yet not clumsy and protective enough for what the mission could possibly mean for an explosive's expert. He grabs an extra vest but ensures that it can be made to extend for at least a person needing a 3XXL fit. The suit is green, so he picks up a can of black spray paint and decides he is going to turn it black as well. "Jackson, you think they have some soft metal strips in the armory here?" asks Aaron as he walks towards the door.

"Probably, they have everything else in this place," Jackson replies shrugging his shoulders.

Jackson and Darwin are both finished at the same time and decide it is time to hit the armory. Walking together through the safe house, Darwin sparks a conversation, "Jackson, all this stuff in here, what do you think they use this place for?" he says looking slightly anxious.

"Man, I don't even want to sit here and guess. You hear about these types of places existing, especially in movies, but to actually see one is a different thing," replies Jackson without even looking at Darwin.

Entering the armory, they notice that Georgi is already dressed and looking at all the weapons in the room. Jackson thinks, "Man, Scott was right, body like that she is sure to catch the enemy's attention."

Georgi turns around and waves at the guys as they enter. "Man, it's a lot of shit in here." she says as the guys walk around the room.

"Zelks, what's your preferred weapon anyway, when you get down on the ground?" asks Jackson while reaching for an HK 433 assault rifle. "I am more of a long-distance support person, I mean if I have to fight up close I will, but I prefer to take them out without them seeing me." She picks up a Mauser Kar 98k. "This right here is my baby, it's fast and it gets the job done," says Georgi as she begins to look for ammo. "I will also be carrying a side arm too, Mark 19 Desert Eagle AE. It's a pocket rocket!" she.

Jackson smiles as she walks away, "It's good to see a woman that can handle that cannon," he calls after her. Jackson grabs a sling for his 433 and goes to another shelf to grab an HK MP5 K as well. Finding the ammo to both his weapons, he sits down on a bench and begins to load magazines for both guns. Looking up, he can see Darwin approaching the bench with his weapons as well. Splinter had decided to go with the military favorite M4A1 and a HK MP7.

"What made you choose the seven over the five?" asks Jackson.

"It just feels better and faster when I think about being outnumbered and having to shoot and run a lot," Darwin says as he fills up his magazines as well.

"How many rounds do you think we need?" asks Darwin after he finishes loading his fifth magazine for his assault rifle. "I always just load the standard battle load, 210 rounds, which is seven 30-round magazines," Jackson says as he finishes all seven of his AR mags. "Also, pack 150 rounds, which is five 30-round mags of 9mm for that SMG as well." Jackson picks up his own magazines. "I'll see you in the command center." Dee says as he rises from the bench and strides out of the room.

Walking into the command center, Jackson glimpses Georgi sitting on the table talking to Scott who was leaning back in his seat with a pile of what looked to be trash next to him.

"Horner, what the hell is that mess?" asks Jackson pointing at the trash pile. Scott stands up and lifts the trash pile off the floor. Instead of it falling all over the place, it's all fitted together into a sort of pullover with a hood and sleeves. "It's my urban ghillie suit," says Scott excitedly. "I figured if Milwaukee is as war-torn as they are making it out, there will be trash and debris everywhere. If the mission calls for it, I blend right in and I can take some good cover shot when needed." Scott forms a gun with his fingers and creates a shooting motion with it. "That's actually great thinking, man," replies Jackson.

Just then Aaron and Darwin walk in. Aaron is carrying what looks to be a heavily modified EOD suit.

"Yo, what did you do to that thing?" asks Scott clearly in amusement.

"Well, since we're going into a city where I'm sure explosives will be used and I might be exposed to some sort of radiation, I modified my suit," Aaron says in a matter-of-fact tone. "Yeah, clearly," fired back Scott looking the suit up and down.

"So, what did you all do to it seriously?" asks Jackson to cut those two off from arguing. "I just added a vest to the front, sewing it on and then on the parts that are not extra protected, I covered with that soft metal and spray painted it all black. I call it the Juggernaut," says Aaron, looking at his masterpiece as he holds it up for the team.

Aaron lays his suit on the ground next to him as he grabbed a seat on the bench next to Darwin. Everyone is now in the room; the meeting can finally begin. "After the team is briefed, Aaron and Scott go grab your loadouts and meet us back in front of the safe house for exfil. Scott stands up and looks at Aaron, "Let us go grab that real quick; that way after the brief we can just head out." He stands awaiting confirmation from Jackson. Jackson nods and allows them to run out to the armory. "You know me, Dee, I am just grabbing my Barrett M82 and MP5," says Scott as he runs through the door, Aaron right on his heels.

After what seems to be only minutes, the men come back into the room. Scott is carrying what he said as he left the room, but Aaron was carrying so much more. Along with his HK MP5 and 433, he also carries loads of loose Semtex and blocks of C4 as well. Jackson points at the Semtex. "What is that for?"

"Using this Semtex, which I like to refer to as puddy, I can wrap my frag grenade in it, add a small blasting cap and bam, grenades that can stick to things when they land," Aaron replies. "Well, I'll be damned," says Scott, raising his hand. "I'll take some of that."

Everyone is finally finished gearing up and ready for the mission brief. Jackson opens the folder and sets it on the table in front of them. "Okay guys, here is what we're going into, and here is what we're going to do to handle it."

around at the team. No one answers. It is settled; Aaron will be the driver once they touch down into Milwaukee.

"Just to reiterate, from Washington High, we make our way to the US Bank Center, recover the chip, rescue the doc if we can, and exfil at Miller Park." Jackson repeated it one more time to the team. The team all nodded, and the mission was a go. "From now on, we go by code names; we are live ladies and gents." He begins packing up the folder and adjusting his gear. "Our comms will be on two-way radio Channel 13." Scott says as he starts to adjust the dial on his receiver. Everyone takes out their receiver and adjusts it accordingly. Jackson adds in his final statement before they head out, "Command post will be satellite comms, Darwin will be radio man and carry the pack for it." Darwin gives a thumbs up, walks over to the desk and grabs the black bag that carries the radio. "This is the Elite Five, lady and gents, and we are officially going dark." Jackson is the last one to file out of the command center and shut the lights off.

11

The elite five exit the safe house and walk outside into a darkness that is as deep as the ocean with almost the same visibility. The only source of light is the moon, a bright yellow that most would call the harvest moon. The lake in front of the building is so static it looks like black glass in the darkness. Just into the woods on the right of the lake the team can hear the engines of the two black SUVs that brought them to the safe house. Just then the lights of both vehicles flash on, the team begins to move towards them.

"Everybody good to go?" asks the secret agent in the driver seat of the first SUV. Jackson looks around and asks, "What happened to that guy that brought us in?"

The driver looks at his partner and says, "We switch shifts every six hours, you guys were in there a long time." Jackson nods and signals his team to move forward and load up the SUVs. When both vehicles are loaded up the driver of the first SUV peers back towards Jackson and says, "POTUS has asked us to take you to BWI where you will board your rides to Milwaukee. From there you will only have comms with the 'Command'."

Jackson nods to show that he understands, and the driver turns and makes a U-turn to drive out of the woods. The other SUV follow behind theirs. The drive to the airport is quiet, the only thing on the team's mind is the mission and if they will see their families again. Getting captured and facing the gulag is not an option, there is a chance that you won't make it out if go in and dying is not in the cards.

Looking out of the window, Georgi is contemplating whether she made the right choice. Her husband would be alone and not knowing if she was safe or not. No communication with family or friends during this mission will make it like no other mission she had completed. Georgi was trying to force panic back when Darwin bumps her with his elbow. "Hey, you good, medic?" he asks her.

She forces a smile and answers, "Yeah, just a little nerves before a mission like always."

Darwin leans back as far as he can with his gear on and nods, "Yeah, I can definitely understand that, but DAAM and Snipez are some of the best at their jobs. Not to mention the SEAL that we have on our team as well. Zero is pretty legit too," he says trying to encourage her.

Georgi smiles, "You left yourself out there Delta. You wouldn't be here if you were too shabby as well," she says bumping him back with her shoulder. They look at each other a little longer before they turn towards their windows and stare out. Still looking out of her window, Georgi murmurs, "I wonder how the other guys are handling the imminent arrival of this mission?"

In the first vehicle DAAM, Snipez, and Zero laugh and talk about past missions that they barely escaped or that they thought were their worst missions ever. Laughing deeply DAAM says, "Man, Snipez here saved my life. Killed the dude that was trying to detonate a bomb on my convoy then shot the bomb in the road before we even got to the spot."

Snipez grins, "It was two of my finest shots," he said. "Took them both out with one shot each." Zero on the other hand tells a story about a marine mission he was on instead of the one he really hated--the one that resulted in two of his friends' deaths and his present paranoia about riding in vehicles driven by others.

The SUVs begin to slow down as they arrived at an unoccupied part of the airstrip. It is on a portion of the runway that is not visible by the soon-to-be passengers still waiting inside of the airport of the red eye flights. DAAM looks at his watch; four in the morning, the sun will be coming up soon. Getting out of the SUV and grabbing his gear he watches his team ready themselves for what is about to happen. Just then, they hear the soft "whoosh" of what appears to be a weirdly-shaped UH-60 Blackhawk. When it touches down, the door slides open and the machine gunner motions them to enter the helicopter.

Turning to look for the agents, DAAM notices that the SUVs are already leaving the airstrip. The realization that they do not exist to the public and the mission is a go just sunk in.

"Oh, we got the best of the best lady and gents," says Zero, shaking the hands of the door gunner. "These guys belong to the Night Stalkers from the SOAR unit out of Fort Campbell. If we got these guys it's serious, but they get the job done." DAAM walks up to the gunner and shakes his hand. "So, what's the plan for landing this bad boy," he says to the soldier. The soldier lifts his goggles and says, "We will fly at low altitude for the whole flight there, once we enter the Milwaukee airspace we will go lower."

DAAM nods and says, "Wouldn't that risk us being seen by the enemy?"

The soldier smiles. "If anyone sees us it won't matter; we're fast and quiet enough to disappear." The soldier continues, "Once we get into the airspace, you will mark your LZ with this green laser and we will put you there." he gives DAAM the laser pointer.

"So, you will do a quick touchdown?" asks Zero. The pilot opens his window and says, "That's a negative, ghost rider. We will hover while you guys rope down."

Zero glances at the other members of his team, "I love a little air assault!" he says. The others agree and the demeanor of the entire team seems to morph into one. It is finally go time.

"Alright, everybody, let's load up!" says DAAM as he enters the helicopter. The rest of the team follows DAAM into the Blackhawk. The gunner takes his seat and slides the door shut. Everyone reaches up and grabs a pair of the headphones hanging above them. Inside the headset the pilot introduces himself. "Welcome aboard, Thunder Cat," he says. "I am your pilot CW4 Lucas at your service. It's time for deployment!" he says before cutting out.

Part 3

The Rush

*"Whether you like it or not, history is
on our side. We will bury you!"*
— Nikita Khrushchev

12

The silenced UH-60 Blackhawk approaches the Milwaukee, WI airspace. "Entering enemy airspace," states the pilot as he begins his slow descent to ensure that he is below radar detection. Looking through the open windows of the helicopter the team takes in the sights of what appear to be a war-torn city. It is almost unrecognizable. The city is bright orange; the color from the fires all around the city brighten the horizon from a deep purple to an eerie orange glow. Plumes of black smoke rise into the air, causing the actual city to burn with an evil dark cloud above like a visual from a horror film.

The helicopter flies past one of the main attractions of the city. What was then the Miller Park Stadium now stands in ruins. The stadium roof is completely blown off, leaving all the metal framing crippled and exposed as if it were a skeletal system exposed after skin is stripped from the bone. All the windows that could be either opened on a nice day or wrap the building shut when it is less than ideal are blown out. Glass and debris litter the inside seating like peanut shells on game day. What the team thinks as a unit is the confirmation of the damnation of the city by the way the stadium's name hangs limply from its perch. The only visible letters left on the stadium read "Mil...P." From the look of the devastation done, the stadium is barely standing, landing on top would not be an option if that field were the designated landing zone for exfiltration.

The pilot's voice perks back up into the headsets of the team, "Get ready for deployment, mark me a landing zone," he shouts into his headset. DAAM takes out the green laser pen that the pilot gave him when he first boarded the helicopter. The machine gunner slides the side door open for DAAM to have an uncontested view of what is left of the city before him.

Just as they agreed in the planning of the mission, DAAM chooses to mark the U.S Bank Center, the tallest building in Milwaukee, the landing zone for the team. "This looks like a good spot," yells DAAM back to the pilot. The pilot changes his course and heads straight for the tall building. On the approach the team notices the giant hole in the side of the building that is billowing huge amounts of smoke into the air. Looking past the smoke, one can clearly make out what is left of an office space that occupied that area.

"Just in case this building isn't stable enough, I am not touching down, you guys will have to rappel out. Copy?" shouts the pilot over the headset. DAAM looked over to the pilot and gives a thumbs up to confirm that he agrees. The machine gunner stands up and walks towards the door with the bundle of ropes in his hand. "On my green light, exit the chopper," he says looking at DAAM and the rest of the team. They all nod and begin to get ready.

The chopper approaches the building with no issues and hovers just over 50 feet above the roof top. "Just got word from Command DAAM, the President has authorized a toxic gas to be dropped in the city. It has already been released at the borders, in 25 minutes the city will be totally engulfed, and anyone left inside will die," calls the pilot over the headset. "GREEN LIGHT! GREEN LIGHT!" yells the gunner as he releases the two ropes out the door. DAAM and Snipez are the first on the ropes, clamped in and already descending the line. Before he can remove his clip from the line, Zero is right behind him followed by Medic on the opposite line. Delta is the last one off the helicopter; the team is starting off in a good position. Delta begins his descent as the Blackhawk starts to receive small arms fire. In momentary surprise, Delta completely forgets to clip his rig to the line and slides down without any protection from falling off the rope. "Shit, that burned," exclaims Delta as his knees buckle under him on his landing. Snipez reaches down and helps him to his feet.

With everyone on the roof now, the helicopter attempts to leave the danger area, but it is now being pounded with bullets from the tail side. Just as the ropes are reined back into the Blackhawk it begins to lift. An RPG flies past the cockpit and connects with one of the U.S Bank Center top floors. The shock wave causes a vibration that makes the team brace against whatever they can on top of the building. Before another rocket can be sent toward the helicopter, the pilot lurches forward and flies out of reach of the incoming bullets. The enemy know they have arrived.

DAAM reaches into his pocket and pulls on his black gloves. It is game time, and he is thinking of the next move. "Alright everyone, give me a sit rep," says DAAM over the headset. The team looks over to him and they all give a thumbs up. The mission is underway. "So much for coming in quietly," says Snipez as he walks up to DAAM. Nodding, DAAM replies, "Yeah, now they know we're here, they will be hunting us down."

Taking out his map, he highlights where their current position is and begins to give the team the next orders. "So, with the new update, we now have less than twenty minutes to get to the doc and secure the chip and the woman for extraction before the gas moves in," says DAAM to the team. "According to the last intel, the doc was being held at the stadium that we passed on our way in" he says, pointing to the stadium on the map. "We need to make our way there and retrieve the package and head for exfil. We can then all rest and be rich with our families when this is over."

The Elite Five stare over the edge of the building and they can see the toxic gas moving in on them—less than a mile away. The clock is ticking. "Delta, get on the comms and radio in for us to receive a UAV on our mark. We need to know who and how many are around us before we leave this building," DAAM says, looking over the edge into the burning city. Delta pulls out the sat phone that is connected to his pack and begins the radio call, "Command this is Elite 5, we need UAV in our location, over."

Waiting for a response, Delta moves over to DAAM. "This is Command, bird is entering a flyover now, you will have visual for four minutes," says a woman's voice over the radio. DAAM pulls out the heartbeat sensor, a new technology he packed for the mission. It is shaped like the old generation iPads, but the display is always in black and white. It receives the feed from the UAV in real time. It offers enemy locations, direction of travel, and if the enemy is in a building, it offers what floor the enemy is on as well. When the heartbeat sensor is not receiving the imaging from the UAV, it can be used to locate enemies in the direction you are traveling within 50 meters based on thermal heartbeat monitoring.

"Listen up, ya'll, we got company early," says DAAM as he points to the only door on the rooftop. "We have a four-man team coming up the steps as we speak, three floors below us." He looks at the heartbeat sensor. Turning to the edge of the building, he notices a few more enemy on the sensor as well. "Once we clear this team," says DAAM, we have to jump down to the building to the south; make sure you pull your close combat chutes, I lost my last CO to him failing to open his." He took position behind the generator ten feet from the door. Hurrying to the door, Zero reaches into his bag and pulls out a block of C4 and begins to plant it on the door handle, inserting the wireless charges to the puddy, "Charges set," says Zero as he backs away from the door and rounds the corner to avoid the blast. Positioned right above the door is Medic, out of her pack she pulls out a small piece of metal, that she immediately begins to expand until it is now four feet by five feet in diameter. She calls it her deployable cover. It is something she took everywhere to give herself instant cover if she needed it. Because of her positioning right above the blast site, the deployable cover will come in handy early.

Still kneeling, Snipez looks up towards Medic and notices a green laser on the cover she is now kneeling behind. Someone has a vantage point on them, and he needs to find them. Grabbing the attention of DAAM, he points to the laser. He points to his eyes, then towards the direction behind them. Creeping around to the edge, he pulls up his sniper rifle to locate the enemy. Scanning the night sky, he sees in the distance across E Wisconsin Ave what looks to be an apartment complex. It is nearly the same height as the US Bank Center but trailed only by 50 feet. Because Medic is at the tip of the building they can see and get a shot on her; but Snipez sees them too.

Looking down his scope, he can barely see the sniper and his spotter. The spotter is constantly moving to the left and right of the sniper trying to judge the wind and distance of the shot. As soon as the spotter steps off to go back around the shooter, Snipez takes his shot. CRACK! Even with a suppressor the .50 Cal is still a loud rifle. Watching through his scope, he knows the bullet travels 1056 feet in a blink of an eye and watches as the head of the shooter explodes and takes the face off the spotter behind him. Both targets down!

13

With the threat behind them neutralized, DAAM preps the team for the combatants moving up the building on them. Looking down at the heartbeat monitor he sees that the enemy is coming up the stairs on their floor. "Zero, on my mark," says DAAM over the headset. Crouching right above the door, Medic is the first person to hear the enemy approaching the door. She points down to the door to signal DAAM that the enemy is in place.

"Now!" yells DAAM to signal Zero. Just then the roof door explodes backwards into the stairwell, DAAM throws two nine-bangers into the stairwell that has now become a fatal funnel for the enemy. BANG! BANG! BANG! The concussion grenade goes off and the screams of the soldiers inside of the stairwell are distinct. DAAM runs into the well after them, two of the combatants are dead while the other two are cowering in the corner, trying to find their way down the steps. "Surprise, muthafuckas" yells DAAM as he fires three shots into each of the remaining soldiers.

Coming back onto the roof the team is already ready to move. "There is a building to our south that is about six stories lower that we can land on. We can re-survey the area from there and begin the track to the stadium." says Zero pointing out the building to DAAM. Nodding in agreement with the plan, DAAM steps up on the ledge, motions for his team to follow, and leaps off the 450-ft building. Immediately he pulls his parachute and glides toward the building they agreed to move to. Following right behind him are Delta and Zero, jumping and triggering their parachutes as well. Medic and Snipez stay back to provide cover as the team moves through the air almost silently.

"Alright, Medic, go ahead I'll cover you," says Snipez. "Just cover me as I come towards you." He motions for her to jump next. "Of course!" she says as she climbs up onto the ledge.

As soon as she prepares to jump, a sniper round hits her square in the chest knocking her backwards into the arms of Snipez. "Medic, are you good? Where did you get hit?" says Snipez as he frantically searches her to look for her wound. Not finding any blood Snipez relaxes and looks Medic in the face.

She's trying to regain her breath. "I didn't know that you cared so much. You know, with us just meeting in all," Medic says with a faint smile on her face. She sits up and the .762 round falls from her chest. The vest stopped the round. Snipez smiled back at her, "I guess you have that effect." He laughs.

Snipez touches his earpiece and calls DAAM over the headset. "DAAM, we are taking sniper fire from a southeast position. Medic was hit, but the vest stopped the bullet, and we are still prepared to jump." From the building that himself and two other members of his team landed on, they are in a worse position than Snipez and Medic are. If they could see and hit them at that height, they could hit them. "Hang tight, Snipez, calling in air strike," says DAAM over the headset.

Looking over at Delta, he signals him to come over behind the roof generator. When Delta makes his run to him, two sniper shots snap against the walls around them. DAAM is right, they can see them on this roof. "Delta, get Command on the sat phone again; we have multiple snipers trained on us and Snipez and Medic on the bank roof." DAAM tries to sneak a peek at the position of the snipers who has them pinned. Delta reaches into his bag to secure the sat phone they used earlier to request UAV around the bank. "Command, this is Delta with Elite 5, over." Waiting for a response, DAAM reaches into his pocket and pulls out the green laser pointer and waves it so Delta can see it.

"This is Command, over," the woman says over the phone.

"We are requesting immediate air support on our position. We are pinned by sniper fire," Delta states over the phone, looking at DAAM. "Predator is circling around, one minute until on location," says Command. Making eye contact with Delta, DAAM nods to let Delta know he is marking the target.

"Target is marked with green infrared laser. Copy?" replies Delta. He is holding the laser on the building where DAAM can see at least three insurgents moving around, the satellite phone perks up with the reply. "Good Copy, target is marked with green laser. Be advised, hellfire cluster strike is inbound," states Command.

Just as the information is passed by command, DAAM can hear the death whistle of an incoming missile. The high-pitched screech of hellfire before impact is sickening when the missile is not coming from allies. Over the headset DAAM calls out to Snipez, "Now is the time to move, cluster inbound."

Snipez and Medic climb the ledge together and jump. Pulling their chutes at the same time, they are high enough to witness the missiles flying overhead towards the snipers. BOOM! BOOM! BOOM! BOOM! BOOM! Five missiles total everything in that area.

Landing in together, Snipez and Medic reach the rest of the team. Looking over the edge, they see the destruction that the cluster of missiles left in its wake.

Standing on the ledge of the building, DAAM checks to see if the enemy might peek and take shots again. Feeling safe, he jumps down and confirms with his team that everyone is good. "Alright guys, let me get a SITREP." he says, glancing at Medic. Zero and Delta both say they are good to go, and only used one magazine of ammo. Medic opens her vest, her curvaceous body exposed underneath but there is no blood. "Just a big bad bruise for now," she says grabbing her breast with both hands and looking at the guys. Snipez smiles at Medic and shakes his head in amusement. Zero and Delta look away and act as if they do not notice the beautiful woman in front of them.

"Good!" says DAAM, as he looks at the sensor to bring up the map of the area. "If we keep moving double-time southeast, we will get to our destination," says DAAM.

Reaching into his pack, Zero brings out five lines to secure on the side of the building to use as zip lines. "I'm going to set these up to make a quick descent from this building," he says. Zero holds the lines up for DAAM to see.

Nodding his acknowledgment, DAAM turns around to look at the rest of his team. "Alright everyone, once we get to the bottom of this building, we are going to move southeast toward the stadium." He glances down at the digital map. "Once we get within a mile of the stadium, Snipez, you will set up on that building about three blocks away. I need you high, you will be our eyes around the stadium and our cover as we move with the package." DAAM points at the building that is on the map. "Zero. Delta," DAAM starts, "I want you two on the ground securing us a vehicle to get out of here in, something roomy but something fast. Medic, you will be with me, we're going in slow and quiet until we have eyes on the package. Once we secure it, all hell will break loose, and we may have to shoot our way out. We have thirty minutes to complete this OP before Washington considers us dead, mission failed, and they hit this city with the bio bomb. Snipez, when you're set, we move on your go. Zero, Delta, secure the vehicle but do not move on us until 15 minutes into the rescue. We want to keep this as quiet as possible until it has to get loud. Once we obtain the package and we hit the vehicles we will rendezvous two blocks east of Snipez location to grab him." DAAM puts his monitor back in his pack and adjusts his gear. "After we grab Snipez, I will call in the rest of our assets. I am dropping the hand of GOD on them! Hellfire and 20mm rounds. Once that dust settles, the bird will pick us up in the center of the stadium. Whatever rat didn't die in that cluster fuck, we will have to fight until extraction arrives. Hooah?" He looks around awaiting his Elite Five to acknowledge the mission.

Snipez chimed in while everyone else replied back with the required "Hooah." "Why does Medic get to go with you? Also, am I providing just overwatch or am I taking these idiots out? He grins a little at Medic. DAAM rolls his eyes before replying, "She's with me because if there is any harm done to the doctor, she has the best skills to assess the damage. She also is carrying the gear that is required for a two-man litter if it is necessary," "As far as your engaging them, take out anyone that you feel would not go noticed while we are inside. If you see two, and you can take them both out before they alert anyone, do it. If not, just inform us of their location and continue to scan," DAAM stared at Snipez to make sure he understood.

"Roger that," Snipez replied.

14

Delta signals to Zero to roll out. Traveling down the road heading east away from DAAM and Medic's location at the makeshift laboratory, they begin taking turns bounding down the road. They cover four city blocks before Zero lifts his fist into the air, signaling a halt on movement. He makes the signal indicating that there are two soldiers in front of him on the left side of the road. Delta looks up from cover and sees the enemy about 50 meters in front of them. Delta rises slightly and runs towards Zero, executing a perfect baseball slide into the kneeling position next to his partner. "Ok, here's what we have," begins Zero, "Two soldiers about 50 meters away. No sign of anyone else or any scouts on the buildings around here." Delta nods in confirmation. "Let's take them out and hide the bodies," says Delta looking up over the car to ensure that the scene hasn't changed. Both men lift their weapons equipped with suppressors. Without giving each other signals they each fire two shots, downing and killing the targets. Moving as a tandem Delta and Zero converge on the dead soldiers. Zero looks around and sees a garbage truck that has been destroyed by the missiles that hit the city. "Let's put the bodies in the back of this truck," he says, pointing at the garbage truck. Both men grab the soldiers by their vests and drag them to the truck. Together they dump the men inside the back. Zero pulls his sling back around the front so his weapon is positioned at the low ready again. "If we keep moving in this direction, I believe there are some vehicles inside of the garage we jumped over on the way to the lab." Zero looks to Delta for confirmation. Delta nods and they begin moving further east towards the garages.

Bounding for three more blocks, Delta and Zero make it to the garage. Entering the building they both instantly freeze and look for cover. Delta looks at Zero and says, "You heard that right?"

Zero nods, peering over the chunk of concrete they are both kneeling behind. "I hear them in here and I hear their radio, but I don't see them," says Zero, trying to case the area without leaving the cover of the concrete slab.

"Yeah, man, I don't know; let's radio Snipez. Maybe he can see from his vantage point." Zero nods and pulls out his radio.

15

"Damn, it is fucking hot up here!" mutters Snipez to himself. "They wonder why I am always a class clown; I get sent alone all the damn time while everyone else has fucking backup." Perched on top of the Milwaukee Veterans Affairs building just a few blocks away from the stadium he can oversee a mile and a half without any restrictions in all directions. This is a perfect spot.

"Snipez come in; over," says Zero over the radio earpiece.

"What's up, pussies?" states Snipez "How can I assist? over."

"Fuck you, man!" mumbles Zero as he continues, "We need you to look over us to see if you can detect how many people are in or on this garage with us; over."

"Yeah, let me get the grids and I will check it out; over," replies Snipez, pulling out his map monitor to input the coordinates.

After giving the coordinates over to Snipez, Zero says, "It's a three story parking garage. We're in the bottom right entrance ground floor."

Snipez gets up and move in the direction of the garage. He instantly spots it, but the reason why is not because the garage was easy to spot. But a garage that has about six men and a bonfire on top makes it that much easier. He gets into prone position and sets up his rifle. While he is screwing the suppressor onto the barrel, he gives Zero the information.

"Alright fellas, this is the deal," he begins. "We have six targets on the roof of the garage. They seem to be burning something on top; over." Snipez doesn't receive any confirmation from Zero, so he continues. "On the south side of the building they have added some sort of zipline. If one of you can take the zip up and the other go up the ramp, we can hit them from three different sides; over."

Zero responds, "Copy, I'll take the zip, Delta will take the ramp; over."

Snipez watches as Zero exits the garage and crouch-runs towards the back of the building just out of his sight.

"Zero," calls Snipez over the radio. "I have no visual of you, but here is the plan. We wait until Delta is in place outside of the roof door. Once he is in place, I will take out the guy closest to the zip and then the guy with the radio. Once you hear the first shot, go up the zip; over." He pauses for a confirmation from Zero. "Roger that, I am hooked waiting on your mark; over," states Zero.

Snipez comes back over the radio but this time speaking to Delta, "Delta, engage the talk button to inform me that you are in position. Once you hear the second shot, come through the door blazing; over."

Delta replies to the command, "Already moving up the ramp, one more floor. Attack on next sound; over." he ends his connection. Silence is all there is to hear in the moments leading into all hell breaking loose on a random roof in a war-torn Milwaukee, WI.

Beep! The chirp from the radio being engaged broke the silence. Snipez lines up the soldier closest to the zipline just above where Zero is waiting to ascend. Boom! Snipez fires one shot that would have been a kill shot if the soldier had not reached over the edge of the building. The bullet penetrated the upper back of the target, shattering his armor plates in his vest and instantly putting him on the ground. Paralyzed! "Fuck!" Snipez exclaims, after realizing he did not kill the target with one shot. He quickly lines up the soldier with the radio and fires his second shot. Snap! One shot down.

Looking through his scope he sees Zero come over the ledge of the roof, he double taps the guy whom he initially hits and turns on the remaining men on the roof. Simultaneously, Delta bursts through the door firing at the men from behind as they are attempting to maneuver for cover from Zero's weapon. As he watches his teammates mow down the opposition, Snipez notices one of the soldiers running for the jeep on the roof trying to make an escape. "Oh no you don't," he mutters under his breath. Re-racking his Barrett .50 Cal rifle, Snipez takes the shot. Penetrating the passenger seat window and instantly silencing the man forever with a head-exploding kill shot. Snipez engages his radio for both of his comrades to hear him, "Team Wipe!" he yells with a hearty laugh.

16

Zero straightens up and readjusts his gear. Looking around, he sees the massacre that just occurred on the roof he is standing on. Teamwork at its finest and he realizes the guys he is on this mission with are definitely the right match. Walking towards the jeep that the last guy attempted to get away in, he notices the keys are in the ignition and the vehicle is in good condition despite the window being blown out and brain matter all over the passenger and driver seat. Reaching the jeep, he throws the body from the seat unto the concrete roof top floor. Noticing the soldier is carrying the same ammo, he takes all ammo from his flak jacket. "You won't be needing these anymore," he states to the dead man. Just then Delta walks up to him, tossing his empty magazine on the floor and inserting a full one back into his weapon. "Well, that worked out perfectly," he says with a smile on his face.

Zero looks over in the general direction from where Snipez might be located. He clicks his radio and begins to speak, "Nice shooting, Snipez. Thanks for the cover; over."

Snipez replies with a simple, "Yessir," and terminates contact.

Looking back over at Delta, he says, "Well, this looks like the perfect getaway vehicle to me. Let's get staged a block away and wait for the call." Delta opens the back door of the jeep and begins to remove everything from the seats and floor. Not paying attention to what he is throwing out, he shuts the door when the seating space is cleared. Zero walks around the back to look at the entirety of the vehicle. He notices that Delta threw out some things that they can use in the escape. "Dude, we can use this, man." He picks up three smoke grenades from the ground, clipping them to his vest. "Shit, I didn't even notice those," says Delta, shaking his head.

Walking along the roof looking for anything else useful for the exfil, Zero notices that there are some makeshift metal plates on the roof of the building near where the zipline was installed. He calls Delta over to assist him, "Yo Delta, give me a hand with this, will you?"

Delta jogs over to see what can do. "I'm going to grab my skill saw out of my go bag; I just need you to hold it while I cut these three plates from this ledge." Taking off his bag, he pulls his saw out and begins to rip the plates from the ledge. "What are you going to use this for?" Delta asks as Zero strips the last metal plate from the ledge. "Let me show you, grab these." He points towards the two remaining plates lying on the ground as he carries one of the plates and his bag back over to the jeep. Delta grabs the two plates and follows him back to the jeep.

"Okay, here's what I'm thinking. It's five of us plus the doc if they can get her out of there," he begins, "This is a five-seater—barely, we are going to have to squeeze in here plus adding another body, where will that person sit?" He picks up two of the metal plates and connects one side to the other so the edges touch. "If I can make a canopy on top that protects my back, I can stand, and the doc can sit in the middle. She'll just have to have my ass in her face for the ride." He climbs to the roof of the Jeep. "It's either that or she walks," he says, laughing at the thought.

"That sounds like a plan to me," Delta says, lifting one of the metal plates to Zero who is now standing on the top of the Jeep Wrangler. Using the mini-welder from his go bag, Zero begins to weld a canopy top protective wall around the back and opening of the Wrangler's rear. Finished, Zero jumps off the roof, repacks his bag, and hops into the passenger seat. "Let's roll before we're next to get sniped out a car."

Delta gets into the driver seat and heads towards the opening, their part of the mission complete. Now they wait.

17

Reaching the outside door of the Miller Park stadium, DAAM lifts a fist into the air to signify halt to Medic who is just trailing behind him. Engaging his earpiece, he speaks over the radio, "Is everyone in place? Over."

Snipez is the first to reply, "Roger, looking over you guys now; over."

Zero replies next, "Enroute to staging point, Charlie Mike; over." Charlie Mike, the universal phonetic alphabet response meaning "Continue Mission." The real meat of the OP was ready to begin. DAAM signals for Medic to follow him inside the door which he finds unlocked and unsecured. Because of the attack on Milwaukee, the stadium is in bad shape. The usual sliding windows that would cover the stadium's opening on the side are totally blown away. From a mile away if you are high enough you can see directly into the stadium with no problem. DAAM sends up a silent prayer that he has the best sniper he knows covering him, looking through those openings. "Snipez, do you have a visual on anyone close to us?" says DAAM over the radio.

Snipez takes his time replying to the question from DAAM. "Looks like you have about three men directly down the hall from you." Snipez says over the radio. "You also have about four more on the floor directly above you standing outside one of the box offices." Snipez finishes his sweep before disengaging the communication button to allow DAAM to reply.

"Roger that!" DAAM states before turning to Medic, signaling with his hands that he has three targets ahead of them. She steps ahead of him as he holds the door open for her to walk through. Approaching through the inner hallways of the stadium DAAM and Medic come to a stop behind a cement pillar that separates them from the three targets about 65 meters in front of them. Two of the men are standing side by side leaning on one of the handrails smoking a cigarette while the third man stands across from them talking. Medic engages her radio, "Snipez, I am in place to take the shot. Can you take the two standing side by side?" she says surveying the area while taking her Kar98k from the sling attached to her back.

Sounding as if he'd taken aback, Snipez replies, "Hell yeah, I can take them both. That's a collat, baby!"

Lifting her rifle to take her shot, she sees that her target notices Snipez' green laser on the side of his companion's black skull cap. It is too late, she fires before he can react, all three men go down together like a threesome of human bowling pins. *Beep*! "Team Wipe" Whispers Snipez over the radio. Medic gives a smirk before looking to DAAM for the next command.

DAAM walks over to Medic and takes a knee next to her. "Okay, the next level is where they are holding the doctor. However, we have no actionable intelligence on where the microchip could be. Hopefully she knows," says DAAM looking at Medic. DAAM pulls out his Heartbeat Senor to scan the area for potential targets enroute to their HVT. Nothing appears on the scan and, knowing that Snipez has confirmed four targets above them, he finds that odd. Looking up from the sensor, he says, "This is weird. Snipez confirms there are four guys above us, however, the Heartbeat sensor isn't picking them up or anyone for that matter."

"They have some sort of ghosting technology that doesn't allow them to come up on this sensor, I'm going to have to call in an Advanced UAV that will give us a heat sig reading of this building." Reaching for his sat phone, he dials the number for the command station, beginning to speak once the line connects, "Command, this is DAAM, we need to have a heat scan UAV above the stadium."

Command replies after about a five second delay, "Friendly UAV inbound. One mike out." Looking at the Heartbeat sensor again, the first sweep of the radar is blank, however the second sweep displays 26 heat indicators on the screen. Quickly doing the math, five of those signatures can be accounted for. Two are himself and Medic, the other three are the fresh bodies in front of him now deceased but obviously still warm. That meant there were 21 bodies in this building and eight of them just above their position. That definitely had to be the room she was in. "How long do we have access to these thermals?" DAAM asks Command over the sat phone.

"The display will be active for three mikes, DAAM; they are live action. When the person moves, so will the signatures. Three minutes!" replied Command. The call was terminated after the voice reiterated three minutes. DAAM looked at his watch and set a three-minute timer on his watch. That's all they had before they would be blind again.

Putting the sat phone back into his bag, DAAM looks over to Medic, "We have three minutes, let's move." Moving rapidly through the lower half of the stadium, DAAM realizes the only way to the box offices is up the elevator. Moving tactically through the open concept of the stadium's first floor he comes to the elevator. It is clearly offline and not being used. Perfect. He pulls out the Heartbeat sensor again to check the location of the thermals before continuing. The four dots on the display move further down the hall but they seem to be coming back towards the room. However, no one is near the elevator. "Okay, we are clear, good thing none of these dudes are cold-blooded," he says reaching for one side of the elevator doors he looks over to Medic, "Grab the other side, we're going up through here." Medic slings her Kar98k around to her back and grabs the other door to the elevator shaft. Lifting his boot to assist with prying the door open, it finally gives and spreads like the Red Sea did for Moses.

Grabbing his zipline equipment from his bag, he rigs it to the elevator cords and attaches it to his belt clip. "Be right on my ass, Medic," he says before hitting the up button and disappearing up the shaft to the floor above. Attaching her rig to the cords, she follows by mimicking his move up the shaft. Swinging his body out of the elevator shaft, he disconnects from the rig and leaves it connected. Medic is swinging in a few seconds behind. "Leave the rig," he says to her quietly. "We don't have time to fuck with that." He continues, pulling out the Heartbeat sensor again to check the area in front of them. He glances at his watch to check on the time: 2:05 and counting remaining before the UAV is gone. The sensor shows the four men 65 meters ahead down the hall. He also notices that the room they are in front of has four heat signatures as well.

"Alright, let's move." He signals Medic to follow him. Moving closely, crouching but with tactical speed down the hall. Their entire left side is exposed to the outside world through the windowless stadium frame. Stopping just 30 meters from the four targets he engages his radio to contact Snipez. "Snipez, can you hear me?" he whispers.

"Loud and clear," Snipez responds.

DAAM peeks around the pillar in front of him and sees the men standing in front of the room. Each man is carrying a submachine gun, probably MP5s—quick and agile, doesn't take much skill to use. He knows his movements must be on point or he risks being slaughtered in this battered stadium. "Do you have a visual on us," he asks Snipez. "Roger that, also the four dudes in front of you," Snipez replies.

"Good! On your laser, we engage," DAAM says, looking over at Medic standing next to him. She drops her MP5 on the sling and swings her Kar98k to the ready position.

Not long after the order is sent to Snipez, DAAM notices the green laser from the Barrett on the back of the head of the man leaning against the handrail. DAAM lifts his HK 433 and fires three shots into the man directly in front of the door. Medic follows with a pinpoint shot to the face of his partner directly to his left. Before the man on the handrail can react, the front of his face explodes onto the last man. Attempting to pick up his weapon which leans against the wall, the other man slips in the blood that has pooled all around him. DAAM rounds the pillar and quickly fires two shots to the man's chest and one in the head: wiping him from this fight. The last target falls to the ground, striking the door behind him. If the gunshots and grunts from the soldiers didn't alert the people inside the room, that blow to the door surely did.

The door opens and another soldier steps into the horror scene in front of him. He instantly goes down with another shot from Snipez. Medic rushes over to DAAM with her MP5 in hand. Stacking on the door, she leans around him and tosses in two stun grenades. The explosion produces instant yelling and screaming from the people inside. Another shot by Snipez whizzes by DAAM into the room. Following the bullet through the door, DAAM sees the target falling that was just dropped by the .50 Cal round. Underneath his body he sees the doctor. *Perfect!* Medic comes in behind him clearing the right side of the room before running to the famous doctor. "Are you okay?" she asks as she physically checks for wounds. The doctor is in good condition as far as she can see, not counting the shock from the stun grenade. Kicking the body out of the way that was lying on top of the doctor, Medic helps the woman to her feet.

"I am sorry to ask this right now, ma'am, but I have to," starts the Medic. "But what is your name and profession?" Medic watches the woman try to reclaim her bearings before answering the question. "My name is Dr. Maria Gonzalez. I am a nuclear scientist, specializing in nuclear warfare." Unconsciously, she attempts to fix her hair.

DAAM walks over to the dead man just inside of the doorway and picks up his radio. The radio chips on and someone speaking a foreign language comes through. "Американцы здесь. У них есть доктор."

"Russians," says DAAM, looking over at the doctor.

She nods, "Yes, and they just said that Americans are here, and you guys have me." DAAM looks at the doctor in shock "You speak Russian?"

"Yes, and a few other languages," she says humbly. Just as they were about to move out, Snipez voice comes over the radio. You guys have the package, but you have a shit ton of company moving up on you." He actually has a hint of excitement in his voice.

Medic grabs the doctor's arm, "Where is the chip?" she says, staring directly into Dr. Gonzalez' eyes. I have it; I was finalizing it when you guys came into the room." She digs the microchip out of her white lab coat. DAAM snatches it away from her. He pulls a small metal box out of his vest upper pouch. Putting the chip into the box, he shoves the box back into the pouch. "Where is the detonator?" he asks as he peeks out the door. Dr. Gonzalez looks at both warriors and with a straight face she says, "There isn't one. You attach it to whatever you want, and whenever that thing explodes, it detonates."

So, if a bullet hits this box and strikes the chip we are nuked?" he says patting the pouch where he has just put the microchip. "Yes, that is what it is made for," she says.

"Stay close, doc, it's about to get real funky out here," says DAAM as he walks out of the room. Medic and the doctor right behind him. "Snipez, what are we looking like?" Medic says over the radio. "It's a shit storm from your left and right. You need to go over the railing and you need to go now," he yells through the radio.

Grabbing the doctor, DAAM hugs her. "Wrap your arms around me and don't let go," he says to her. Without question she does what she is told. Moving to the railing they climb to where he stands on the top and she has her arms hooked around his neck and legs around his waist. "Trust me," he says to her. DAAM looks over to Medic who has climbed the handrail as well to his left. Locking eyes, they nod.

He jumps.

Part 4

The Final Circle

"Victorious warriors win first and then go to war, while defeated warriors go to war first and then seek to win."
-Sun Tzu

18

Pulling his combat parachute, DAAM and Dr. Gonzalez begin to glide across what used to be the Milwaukee Brewers outfield. Hearing her chute behind them, he knows that Medic was able to successfully jump and pull her combat parachute as well. Through his earpiece he hears Snipez' voice, "multiple targets are at the rails you guys just left. Got to cut those chutes or you will be shot out of the air." Before he terminates the connection, DAAM and Medic hear him fire two shots. Trusting his team, he pulls the knife out of his belt. "Hard landing, Doc," he says before he cuts the cords attaching him to his parachute. Twelve feet above the ground, the landing is not soft, especially for Dr. Gonzalez. "Ahhhhhhhhhhhh," she screams as she makes contact with the ground. Medic and DAAM hit the ground and execute a combat roll almost simultaneously. Medic gets up and runs towards her, grabbing her by the shoulders and dragging her to the closest cover she can find. Some of the steel ceiling from the roof is all over the field. This is perfect for cover from bullets, which begin to rain down on them from all angles. DAAM runs towards her and the doctor.

"What's the assessment? DAAM says to Medic as he dives behind the metal framework they are using as cover. "Compound fracture in both her ankles. She's not going to be able to walk out of here."

"Fuck!" he says out loud. "Okay, Plan B."

"What the fuck is Plan B, DAAM?" Medic says with a look of actual concern in her eyes. DAAM gets on the radio and yells over cracks of gunfire, "DELTA! ZERO! WE NEED THAT CAR ON THE FIELD NOW!" Hearing no response, he yells the command again. "Medic, get her splinted. Snipez, and I will return fire. Yell when you're ready to move."

Medic looks at him, "Move where? We will be gunned down as soon as we leave from behind here. They are everywhere."

"Just do what I said; we can't fucking stay here, he exclaims." She shakes her head, rips her bag off her back and goes to work on the doctor.

DAAM takes a peek over the metal frame and looks at the execution squad all around him. There is no way they are getting out of this situation. He mounts his weapon and begins firing into the crowd of men rushing the field on the bottom floor towards their position. Then Dr. Gonzalez screams and points behind Medic's head. Medic picks up her MP5, rolls right into a kneeling position and with what seems like aim assist, empties her 30-round magazine into the three men running towards them from behind. She scurries back to the doctor to finish wrapping her splints. "DAAM, they are moving in behind us too," Medic says, looking up at the back of him while he continues to fire rounds down range.

He turns and sits down, ejecting his empty magazine onto the ground before loading another custom 60-round magazine. "This is a fucking shitstorm!" he yells before getting back to his knee and firing down range again. "This is the best I can do at the moment, Doc. Here is some morphine for pain," Medic says to the doctor before injecting her with the pain medication. "DAAM! Ready to move!" she yells. He turns and drops to the seated position again. "They are like forty meters from us, no way we outrun them. We may be fucked here, Medic." He shakes his head.

To their left, they hear a loud explosion, then the engine of a vehicle rushing towards them from right field. Looking up over the frame, DAAM sees the enemy turn around and begin firing on a Jeep Wrangler moving fast towards them. "Fuck yes!" he yells.

"Our ride is here," he says, looking back at Medic and the doctor. He reaches to his belt and unclips two more stun grenades and heaves them towards the group of men now firing towards the other two members of his squad. The grenades detonate sending a blinding light and five loud bangs towards the men in the open field. The firing ceases but the Wrangler continues to move. DAAM ducks behind the metal once again and runs over to the doctor. Both him and Medic pick up the doctor and get her ready to board the vehicle. As they crouch in wait, they hear the men scream, shots being fired close and then the sickening crunch as the Jeep makes contact with human bodies. Coming to a screeching halt next to them, Delta and Zero jump out of the Jeep. DAAM and Medic both walk over to the car while Delta and Zero return fire to the new wave of men entering the field. Zero reaches to the back of the Wrangler where a spare tire usually sits and unstraps an AT4 Rocket Launcher. Loading the launcher, he yells, "Back blast area all clear?"

Delta yells back, "All Clear!" Zero fires the rocket into the third-floor box offices where DAAM and Medic have just jumped from. The rocket-propelled grenades explode on contact and bring the third floor down on the hoard of men running onto the field. The men begin to run in different directions to avoid being crushed by the falling third floor.

With the extra seconds DAAM and Medic are able to secure the doctor in the middle back seat. Medic hops into the driver seat and yells, "Let's fucking go!"

Zero reloads another RPG into the AT4, climbs onto the roof and drops his legs into the jeep, straddling the doctor. "Sorry Doc, it's going to be an uncomfortable ride," he says down through the roof of the Jeep. Barely audible because of her pain and the medicine taking effect, she mumbles, "As long as I live, I don't care."

Jumping into the passenger seat, DAAM took the lead. "Zero, you're going to use that AT4 to make a hole, right?" asks DAAM.

"Roger that," he yells, pounding on top of the metal frame he rigged to the roof of the Jeep. Delta slides into the seat next to Dr. Gonzalez. "Let's go!" he says grabbing Medic's shoulder. Before he could get the door closed all the way, Medic slams on the gas and launches forward. Speeding across the outfield of Miller Park stadium, bullets fly all around them. Delta sticks his HK 433 out of the window and begins to shoot back. Getting closer to the wall leading into the bottom floor of the stadium, Zero takes aim and launches another rocket towards the wall. *BOOM!* The rocket makes a clean hole in the wall that provides them just enough room to slip through. Speeding straight through the halls of the first floor, men begin to appear in front of them. "RPG!" yells Zero from above. Medic sees him directly in front of them, there is nowhere for them to go in this tight tunnel of a hallway. They are doomed.

19

The man with the RPG is standing directly in front of them as they speed towards the group of men. Medic is within 100 meters of the man when his entire head explodes from his shoulder and the RPG is fired into the ground. *BOOM!* The soldiers next to him are either killed or knocked unconscious by the explosion. Snipez' voice comes over everyone's earpiece, "Headshot!" he shouts. "Keep driving forward at about 50 meters you will come to a down ramp on the left. Take it, it carries you to the parking area which leads outside. Once you enter the parking area, I won't be able to see you anymore. I'll be leaving my perch now. Pick me up three blocks southwest of you."

"Fuck, that was close," Medic says. "I think I love that man now." She laughs. Speeding through the tunnels, she sees the ramp, makes a sharp left, and flies down the ramp. Driving through the stalls of the parking garage, she sees the light at the end, signifying they are almost outside of the stadium. "Almost out of here, fellas," she yells.

Delta hears to his right another set of tires screeching across the cement floor of the parking lot. "We've got company," he yells to his team. Zero sees the vehicle, a blacked-out SUV with a turret gun attached to the roof. "Contact left!"

The turret gun jumps into action, sending rounds towards them in a hurry. Medic begins to swerve left and right—bullets smack against the Jeep.

"Get them off of us," screams DAAM from the passenger seat. Delta begins returning fire to the SUV, causing them to swerve in and out as well.

Medic launches out of the tunnel into the chilly air of Milwaukee and immediately turns right, heading in the direction of Snipez—the SUV right behind them. Reloading the AT4, Zero takes aim and fires the rocket. The projectile makes contact with the ground directly in front of the SUV, exploding, causing the SUV to somersault into the air and land onto its roof on fire.

"Good Shit," yells Delta. DAAM looks at Medic and tells her to stop the Jeep. He gets out and pulls out his laser. Using his sat phone, he calls Command. "Command, this is DAAM. Requesting Cluster strike on green laser; over," Command responds, "Hellfire missiles inbound." DAAM holds the green laser on the stadium until he can hear the scream of the missile inbound towards the target. He gets back into the Jeep and smacks the dashboard, "Get us out of here," he shouts.

Behind them four rounds of missiles make impact with everything around the stadium. Giant explosions and the ground rumbling are evidence that danger is still all around. Reaching for his earpiece, DAAM calls to Snipez, "Snipez, where are you?" Snipez answers immediately, "Make the next right into the alley; I'm there, I can hear you coming." Making the right into the alley, Snipez comes from behind the tall building to their right. He jumps into the backseat on the other side of Dr. Gonzalez. Medic speeds off.

"What's up with the Doc?" yells Snipez pointing his thumb in the direction of the doctor. "Both ankles shattered and highly medicated. She's probably fainted," says DAAM, looking over his shoulder towards Snipez.

"Damn, that's shitty," he says, looking over at the doctor. Medic glances at DAAM, silently asking what the next move is.

"Evac is at the stadium; that's why I called the Cluster strike there. Trying to clean it up for our return."

DAAM says to Medic, "Let's head back that way."

She puts the Jeep in reverse, steering them out of the alley. Turning right, she speeds back towards the stadium.

20

eading back north in the direction of the stadium DAAM and Medic spot two more blacked-out SUVs at the end of the street. He locks eyes with the driver of one of the vehicles. "Turn right here," he orders Medic. "How the fuck did they make it out of that?" she says as she whips the Jeep to the right and speeds down the street. Turning around in his makeshift turret hole, Zero notices that both SUVs are following them. "Step on it, Medic, they are on our ass." He yells down into the Jeep, "Zero, take them out," orders DAAM. Already loaded up, Zero aims the AT4 at the first SUV behind him. He fires the rocket launcher, and the SUV instantly turns down another street to its right. The rocket is then exploded in midair. The second SUV emerges from the explosion unscathed from the rocket.

"Trophy system!" yells Zero. Delta reaches into his pack and pulls out three frag grenades. He opens his door pulls the pins and rolls the three grenades out of the Jeep down the road towards the SUV. They look like deadly bowling balls. As the SUV rolls over the grenades, they explode, launching the SUV into the air and disabling the vehicle.

"Second vehicle down," Delta yells shutting his door.

Looking to his right, DAAM tenses up as he notices another SUV coming at them as they are crossing through an intersection. He raises his rifle and fires his weapon. Shattering the windshield and dropping the driver and passenger of the SUV. "Downed two of them out of the vehicle," he says as the SUV stops moving and the Jeep continues to move forward. Making a left at the next intersection they begin the scary trip back to the stadium.

"Delta, call in our evac, yellow smoke will be the designator."

"Roger that," says Delta as he reaches into his pack to grab the radio. "Come in Command; over."

After a quick pause a woman's voice responds, "This is Command; over." Delta engages the radio, "We are requesting evac, Break. LZ will be marked with yellow smoke, Break. Package is secured, how copy? Over."

"Good copy. Yellow smoke marks LZ. Bird is in the air. 20 mikes out." Command terminated the connection.

"Twenty minutes until are back home everyone. Look alive!" Delta says to his team.

Snipez looks out of his window into the sky. Hearing the tell-tale rotation of helicopter blades, he looks over to Delta and asks, "I thought you said twenty minutes?" A black helicopter with three soldiers sitting on the sides appeared from behind a building, tailing them from the sky. "Yeah, they're not with us!" yells Zero. The two men on the left side of the helicopter begin firing down towards the Jeep. "Fuck, get us out of here, Medic," shouts DAAM as he begins to return fire to the helicopter. Delta turns around in his back seat and starts to shoot back at the chopper as well. Loading the AT4 with his last rocket, Zero takes aim at the helicopter. Firing the rocket launcher, he throws the AT4 and grabs his MP5. The helicopter dips left and evades the rocket, causing the missile to hit a nearby building, crumbling it on impact.

Getting back into position, the helicopter begins shooting at them again. This time connecting. Two bullets hit the doctor in the chest and put her into a sleep from which she will never wake up. The bullet also completely goes through Zero's left leg, shattering his shin, causing him to stumble and drop his weapon. In pain, Zero reaches to his waist and grabs his Desert Eagle and continues to shoot at the helicopter. Snipez grabs Medic's shoulder to get her attention. "When I say so, turn right, ok?" he says. She nods her confirmation and continues to swerve down the road. The helicopter switches sides to allow the one man to fire his weapon while the other two reload. This guy hits his target.

21

While Delta is reloading, he glances at his watch. "Five minutes until evac!" he shouts. Delta turns to engage the helicopter after reloading and is hit with two shots in the face. Instant death, Delta's body slumps into the back seat, no longer responsive.

"Fuck me, Delta is down, he's gone, DAAM," Snipez yells, reaching over the body of the doctor. The helicopter moves back into its original position now that the other soldiers have reloaded, and they begin to fire at the Jeep again. This time both men focus on Zero, riddling his body with too many rounds to count, causing his body to lay limp over the roof of the Jeep. "FUCK!!" shouts Snipez. Zero is done."

DAAM grabs the yellow smoke grenade from his vest and launches it out the window straight ahead of him. It rolls into the parking lot of the stadium located right in front of them. "Medic, turn now!" screams Snipez. Medic takes the last street on the right before the opening to the stadium. Taking the helicopter by surprise the chopper executes a wide turn to follow the Jeep. Snipez was counting on the pilot to make that mistake. Already aiming down his scope, he fires his shot as soon as the helicopter levels out. The bullet shatters the windshield, making contact with the pilot. Snipez turns around in his seat facing forward again. "Downed the pilot," he says shaking his head.

The helicopter instantly takes a nosedive into the building to its right, exploding on impact. Turning left, Medic heads towards the yellow smoke. For the second time, they hear the sound of a helicopter, but this time it is friendly. Pulling into the yellow smoke, what is left of the team exits the Jeep. DAAM and Snipez together drag the bodies from the vehicle and lay them side by side. "We're not leaving them," DAAM says to Medic and Snipez. "They helped us complete this mission. Without them, the Doc, myself and Medic wouldn't have made it."

"Wouldn't have even thought about leaving them, bro," says Snipez, putting his hand on DAAM's shoulder. Medic just nods silently, looking at Delta and Zero—two men that saved her life.

The chopper gets into position over the team, lowers four ropes, and drops three litters from the cabin of the helicopter. Putting Zero on the first litter, they strap him in and connect two ropes to the litter. The men in the chopper pull the litter up to the chopper. Waiting on the two ropes to return, they do the same thing to the other two bodies, Delta and Dr. Gonzalez. Loading Delta next, they watch him get lifted into the chopper before the soldiers drop the ropes back down for Dr. Gonzalez.

Snipez connects his rig to the rope and zips up the rope into the helicopter. DAAM watches Snipez zip up to the chopper and he remembers that Medic and himself left their rigs in the stadium. DAAM touches his earpiece, "Snipez, let them know that we will just attach down here, and they will have to pull us up as we're leaving. We don't have our rigs."

Snipez sticks his thumb up. DAAM and Medic strap themselves to the rope and the helicopter begins to take off.

As they lift off the ground, DAAM hears the crack of a sniper rifle and gets splattered with blood as Medic takes a shot in the right shoulder. The helicopter lurches forward to try to get away from the shooting when another round connects with her cord, separating Medic from the helicopter. DAAM reaches down and grabs Medic by the vest. Holding on the helicopter, they finally get out of range of any shooter left at the stadium. "Hold on, Medic," DAAM shouts over the loud rotors of the helicopter. Forgetting that he had the radio from the dead Russian soldier at the stadium, the chirp of the radio coming alive startled him into almost dropping Medic.

Static is the only thing he heard over the radio for what seemed like an eternity. Then a raspy but very American voice came over the radio. "This isn't over. America will pay!"

DAAM let that final message sink in. Why was there an American working with Russians and what did he mean that we will pay? The men in the helicopter, along with the help of Snipez, finally manage to bring them into the cabin of the chopper. They attend to Medic and check DAAM to ensure that he wasn't hit as well. Looking over the edge, he sees the city's destruction fading in the distance along with what remains of the yellow smoke that signaled their getaway. Accepting and completing this mission along with what was said over the radio he knows that this won't be the last Black OP he does with what remains of this team. Losing two soldiers and a civilian doesn't seem like a win, but Washington will consider this to be a successful mission because the microchip was recovered. Not liking to lose anyone on missions, DAAM would never consider this to be a win, but according to POTUS he knows they will say this is a great WARZONE VICTORY!

EPILOGUE

D ee Jackson steps out of his Range Rover dressed in an all-black suit. Arlington, VA is very nice this time of year. The leaves have all changed, causing the cemetery to look like a vivid oil painting in the background. The ride here was elaborate, hundreds of cars in the motorcade. Friends, families, colleagues, government officials, including the President of the United States, are in attendance. People from all over have come to witness the funeral of two great people who gave the ultimate sacrifice for their country. However, these people will not know how their lives were truly lost. Only a small group of people will ever know the truth behind the loss of Aaron Luper and Darwin Splinter. Two amazing servicemen protecting the country from a threat that its people didn't even know existed.

Dee walks over the long stretch of green grass, which underneath, houses the bodies of other fallen warriors from past wars. The graves are all uniform, perfectly aligned and not one blade of grass out of place. "Jackson!" calls Georgi, lifting one hand in the air, signaling him to walk towards her. Lifting his hand to acknowledge her presence he moves in her direction. Georgi walks over and gives him a one-armed hug; the other arm was in a sling from a mission that cost Aaron and Darwin their lives. Returning the gesture and looking at her shoulder, Dee asks, "How's that healing up?"

"Couldn't be better," she says shrugging and wincing a little at the pain. "Couple more months in this thing and I'll be alright." She finishes, stepping aside to let Scott pass. Dee smiles, "Good." He reaches out to take Scott's hand. Shaking hands, the two men pull closer for a hug and both men slapped each other on the back. "Glad to see you looking good, man," says Scott.

Dee nods and says, "You don't look too bad yourself, man. Hanging in there?" They move towards the three seats in the front row. Scott shrugs and nods, "Yeah, I guess. Same shit different day." He continues smiling. Reaching their seats, they see the two caskets, both dark brown with eccentric designs. Good taste for outstanding men.

"So," Scott begins, "what's the verdict on the death of these two guys, according to the White House?" he asks, eyeing Dee for an answer. "According to them, they were meeting up in Milwaukee for a few drinks and catching up from a past mission together. Suddenly the city was attacked, and a missile found them." Dee shook his head. "Darwin was still active duty, right?" asks Georgi. "Yeah, I believe so. I don't even think they knew each other before this mission." Dee looks at where the two men will now lay forever.

Glancing across the aisle from where they are sitting, Dee notices two guys that he served with during his time in the Delta Force. Diego and Parker are standing on either side of the President. Are they a part of her detail? Pulling his eyes away from them, he looks at the front where the service has begun. Darwin and Aaron were receiving a full-fledged military funeral. The Chaplain begins his service talking about the men and saying his blessings, casting what he hopes to be his prayers, sending them to Heaven. A few family members and friends come up to speak about each man. It is hard to sit through these for Dee, he has been to too many of these services, and they never get any easier.

The last family member of Aaron leaves the podium, and the President stands and walks towards the stand. She is trailed by both Parker and Diego who take their posts on either side of her. She begins to speak, "I am here today not only to mourn and appreciate the lives of two great men, but also to shed light on the courage these two possessed. Not only during their time of service--which they served with grace and humility—but also with great bravery and patriotism. We all know of the feats Aaron Luper and Darwin Splinter achieved while serving in the Navy and Army respectively, but I am here to talk specifically about what they did in Milwaukee, WI, where they paid the ultimate sacrifice." She continues looking over the crowd.

Turning her page to her speech, President Christian Thomas continued with what appeared to be a tear in her eye, "Aaron and Darwin were seen attempting to rescue and secure as many citizens as they could during the attack on that city. Assisting the MPD with trying to hold back the surge of terrorists from driving the city into destruction. For these valiant efforts it is seen fit to award both men with the Medal of Honor." She pauses in honor. "Both men exemplified gallantry in action, selflessness, unwavering devotion, and extraordinary heroism in the fight against terrorism in our own backyard. Thank you for your service and thank you for paying the ultimate sacrifice for us to live freely." She closes her notes and looks up directly at Jackson and what remains of his team.

As soon as the President steps away from the podium the 21-gun salute begins. "Port Arms; Ready Aim; Fire," orders the Honor Guard Staff Sergeant. Everyone in the crowd rises to their feet to show respect and support for the last time as a group. After the third iteration, the Honor Guard Sergeant orders, "Present Arms." On cue, TAPS begins to play. A line forms, allowing the Navy Seals and soldiers that served with the men to approach the caskets and say their goodbyes. Each Navy Seal tapes Aaron's casket, sealing the golden Navy Seal crest into his casket. Dee is next to come in between the graves and under his breath he whispers, "Thank you for your sacrifice and allowing us to come home. We will never forget. You have now been RTB for retaking to Heaven's Army. Hooah."

Looking up, he sees Parker waving to him to come over to where the President is waiting. Shaking hands with Parker and Diego, Dee asks, "What's this about, and when did you two start working for her?" Diego laughs, "I go where the action is, you already know that."

President Thomas walks over to the group of men and extends her hand to Jackson as she reaches the group. "I hope you are well, Jackson, but I will warn you. This is not over." She looks him directly in the eye. "We lost two good men in this fight. Expect a call from me before too long."

She walks away, not looking back as she storms towards her entourage. Parker reaches for Dee's hand again, "Good seeing you, man, and from the sounds of it, we will be seeing you again." Dee nods and let's go of Parker's hand before reaching out to shake Diego's. Both men follow behind the President.

Returning to his friends, Scott and Georgi, he fills them in on what the President just said to him. "Apparently the threat isn't over." He stares at his friends. "She said she will be calling me soon, well 'seeing' me soon is what she actually said." Georgi puts her good arm on top of her head, "No way am I doing this shit again. I'm sorry, Dee, but after that shit in Milwaukee, she can count me out." She shakes her head determinedly. Dee looks over to Scott to see if he has any comments. Scott grins, "Man, you know I'm with you if you need me; wish Georgi would bring her tight ass with us but I know she probably has men waiting back home that deserve it more than this country does." He gives a hearty laugh, patting Georgi on her back.

"Roger that," Dee says. "I'll keep you informed." He hugs his two friends and walks back to his SUV. Sitting in his driver seat, his phone chirps with a new text message. The number that appeared on the screen is unfamiliar, so he opens the message. "I know who you are, DAAM, and this isn't over." He stares at the screen for a few seconds, drops it into his passenger seat and puts the car in gear. Driving away, he thinks, *"Try me motherfucker, gulag is no option for you."*

CPSIA information can be obtained
at www.ICGtesting.com
Printed in the USA
BVHW060614011221
622870BV00006B/497

9 781977 249081